There has never been a rat like Doctor Rat, Ph.D. Frenzied survivor of medicine's most vicious experiments; brilliant eunuch; insane prophet of progress through genocide.

DOCTOR RAT

is sheer horror, pure joy, a one-rodent crusade. He's man's best friend . . . Nature's worst enemy . . . and the world's maddest Messiah. He's an experience you'll never forget.

"Bill Kotzwinkle is one of the few American writers who is in complete control of his materials and his materials seem to come from somewhere deep down . . ."

—Kurt Vonnegut, Jr.

DOCTOR
RAT

—

William Kotzwinkle

BANTAM BOOKS
TORONTO · NEW YORK · LONDON

RLI: $\dfrac{\text{VLM 8 (VLR 5–8)}}{\text{IL 9+}}$

DOCTOR RAT
*A Bantam Book / published by arrangement with
Alfred A. Knopf, Inc.*

PRINTING HISTORY
*Knopf edition published May 1976
Bantam edition / September 1977*

Portions of this novel originally appeared in REDBOOK *magazine.*

ISBN 0–553–10382–2

Published simultaneously in the United States and Canada

*Bantam Books are published by Bantam Books, Inc. Its trade-
mark, consisting of the words "Bantam Books" and the por-
trayal of a bantam, is registered in the United States Patent
Office and in other countries. Marca Registrada. Bantam
Books, Inc., 666 Fifth Avenue, New York, New York 10019.*

PRINTED IN THE UNITED STATES OF AMERICA

Doctor
Rat

In the colony I'm known as Doctor Rat. Having been part of this laboratory so long and having studied so carefully, it's only right I be given some mark of distinction other than the tattoo on the inside of my ear, a mark that all the other rats have too. Some of them have tattoos and V-shaped wedges cut out of their ears. Some even have three or four wedges cut out of their ears, but that doesn't mean they are as learned as I. It simply means they have had the liver removed (one wedge), the liver and pituitary gland removed (two wedges), liver, pituitary and pineal glands removed (three wedges), and so forth. After they remove your heart, no more wedges are needed, ha ha!

Then they just bottle your bones, bottle your bones.

But I've come to enjoy the smell of formaline—a 5% solution is satisfactory for removing all the soft parts of a rat's body. Yes, the smell is pleasing to my nose because I know the bones aren't mine.

From my platform here in the maze, I can watch the whole procedure—a dead rat is now being dunked in the formaline. Soon all the soft parts of his body will fall away. Then a simple solution of sodium carbonate, bleaching powder, and water is sufficient to take off the rest of any muscles or fat left hanging. The expense is not great. To the rat involved, of course, the expense is complete, but what does he care, he's free!

Death is freedom, that's my slogan. I do what I can for my fellow rats, giving them the best advice.

1

For after all is said and done, the Final Solution (5% formaline) is death, and death is freedom.

My own case is not unusual. I was driven mad in the mazes. The primary symptoms of shivering, whirling, and biting have all passed now, but I've been left with the curiously mad practice of writing songs and poetry. Obviously this is somewhat out of place in a scientific atmosphere and I do my best to suppress the tendency, giving all my attention to writing learned, factual papers. I like to think they're the very latest word in animal behavior.

Well, why shouldn't they be? I am intimate with all the animal behavior programs. There's an interesting demonstration going on in the lab at the moment: A young rat has just been placed on a small metal stand. His back paws have been pierced by thumb tacks which hold them in place nicely; his front paws are raised onto the metal stand and tied there, so he'll remain in an upright position. His eyes dart about. I can feel the racing of his heart, and I call to him, giving him moral support.

"Don't worry, fellow rat, it won't take long."

"What are they doing to me!"

"Nothing that won't be done to all of us, sooner or later, dear brother. Remember the slogan, death is freedom."

"I don't want to die!"

The Learned Professor who directs the many and varied experiments in our lab has now stepped up to the stand. Carefully, coolly, he makes the cisternal puncture, draining out the rat's spinal fluid. The rat wants to die now, I assure you.

Death is freedom, brother!

Now bottle his bones, bottle his bones.

His spinal fluid is being examined by one of our graduate assistants and now the assistant is pouring it down the sink. He's getting better at this experiment. It's part of my work to spot the promising young scientists and feature them in my Newsletter. At first, this lad's hands were nervous and trembling. He looked a little like a young rat about to be castrated—those weighing more than 30 grams are discarded at birth.

But after practicing on fifty-two rats, the boy is really solid. With a smile of accomplishment he washes out his test tube.

Now over here, in a thermos bottle of ice, you'll see several young rats being cooled to two degrees below zero centigrade.

"Doctor Rat, we're f-f-f-freezing!"

"That is correct, my friends, and soon you'll be c-c-c-castrated, as I am. But you won't feel a thing. Your nuts will be numb and they'll come off without a hitch."

"Please, Doctor Rat, h-h-h-help us!"

"My dear friends, don't worry. After your b-b-b-balls are removed, you'll get your p-p-p-picture in the Newsletter, and it goes all over the world."

In this way, I spread good cheer throughout the lab, helping my fellow rats to understand the important role they play in global affairs.

I should now like to sing "Three Blind Rats." It's part of the experimental program of music that's being channeled toward certain rats, to make them more docile and sweet. Several of them are indeed beginning to nuzzle up to each other, one of them even executing a light-fantastic tripping of his tail, in time to the beat.

In the cage beside them, we actually have three blind rats. In fact, we have twenty-three blind rats, part of a magnificent new experiment initiated by a very ambitious student, whom I'm featuring in this month's Newsletter. He's a sensitive chap and it was his exquisite sensitivity that caused him to dream up the item that's become the latest rage here at the lab: the fabulous removal of the eggs from a female rat's body and the grafting of them to different parts of a male rat's body —to the tail, to the ear, to the stomach. And for the past twenty-three days, he's been grafting them to their eyeballs! So now it's time we sang that promising young scientist a song. I'm stepping to the center of the maze and climbing the Reward Ladder from which I can be clearly seen by all.

"Brother and Sister Rats, members of the choir, I should like us all to sing 'Three Blind Rats,' as part of our research program. Sing:

Three Blind Rats
Eyeballs gone
See how they run
See how they run
We all run after the graduate life
And cut off your balls with a carving knife
Did you ever see such a grant in your life
For Three Blind Rats!"

The voices of the rats in the Hemorrhagic Sore Cage are truly well trained. You will observe one of them being pickled in a few moments. If left too long in the Final Solution the smaller bones will disintegrate. But if taken out in time, they can be scraped and brushed until they're shining clean, and the Learned Professor likes to see that. Good clean bones every time. It gives him the feeling of a job completely and thoroughly done.

Where was I? Oh yes, that young man with the rat's eyeball. He's undoubtedly going to have one of the most unusual papers of the year. It ranks with removing the stomach and connecting the esophagus with the duodenum.

Is that a scream I hear? Oh do, oh do, oh do, oh duodenum, with decapitation as the terminal procedure. I want every one of you to make sure that you die calmly, without any show of fear or twitching, in order that the young scientists will be able to dispense with you neatly and quickly. Remember X-rays can be taken of the rat after its sacrifice by slicing the head with a sharp saw or razor, after which we'll be cutting up your carcass into four parts with a cleaver.

Isn't that a scream?

Is that a scream I hear?

Yes, it is, just down the row of cages. Shall we move along and take a few notes?

"Help, help!"

"Please, young fellow, there's no need to get so worked up about your little contribution to science. Have a bit of pressed biscuit before you die. Eat hearty and remember—death is freedom!"

"What are they doing to me, Doctor Rat?"

"Let me just check my notes . . . yes, here we

are. You'll be the tenth rat this week to have his brains sucked out by a pneumatic tube."

"Help, help!"

I comfort my fellow rats where I can. It requires psychological understanding, of course. And having been driven insane, I hold the necessary degree in psychology.

We all smelled it. Every dog in the area suddenly had it in his nose. I was outside, just taking my morning run. My master had always let me have this, an hour or so when I might roam around the neighborhood, but always within whistling distance. Whenever I heard that whistle I went running back, for a delicious bone. But this morning it was different.

There are many smells in the world, some good, some bad, but there is only one smell like this, only one smell that absolutely cannot be denied, so sweetly satisfying is it.

It isn't a smell from the gutter or from food or from the heat of a female; it isn't from plants or water or rich black soil. I was padding along down the alleyway when I realized it was in the air. Where was it coming from? I lifted my nose, turned slowly around, finding its direction.

I followed it. Not to follow would have been impossible. I dropped everything and ran. Marvelous bones, hearty breakfasts, loving caresses—none of them could compare to this scent, so familiar and yet so fleeting. Don't lose it, don't lose it, any of you. Smell it now—there, around the corner, there, down the street, keep after it, keep chasing, keep picking it out from all the other smells. You must go through fire and water to stay with this scent.

Through the town—out of alleyways and along the streets, back into the alleyways, twisting, turning. There are certain smells that resemble this, but only vaguely, and lacking the overwhelming authority that speaks to us now. The smell of burning candles, the

smell of a river at dawn—these are weak approxima-
tions, but they do suggest a smell whose nature is made
up of the most tantalizing promises which are only
hinted at in the candle's delicate burning and the river's
vagrant mists. It seems to me now that I have, from
puppyhood on, caught a touch of this smell, whose
touch opened secret chambers in my heart. But before
I could dash into those chambers the smell was gone
and I was left standing by a can of garbage, or in a
pile of wet leaves, calling myself a dreamer.

Am I dreaming now?

On every side of me, in gathering numbers—
dogs, dogs, dogs! We're at the edge of the city, racing
along through the last broken streets where poor and
hungry dogs join us from small tarpaper shacks.
They're skinny, snappy creatures, but their spirit is
as high as that of the finest pedigree among us, of
which there is also a great number.

Yes, there are sparkling collars and jingling tags
of every sort. The society dogs as well as the mongrels
are drawn by this powerful lure. Together, all of us
together—oh, it's wonderful as we pad along, tails
wagging, noses lifted, and the smell all around us.

There are the hounds up ahead. They've reached
the meeting place first, hounds of every kind, running
back and forth in the vacant lot at the end of town.
Their noses are to the ground, and they're barking at a
creature who is swifter than any fox or rabbit, a creature who can't be seen, whose scent alone decrees that
he is here. The beagles howl and chase in circles,
the bird dogs point in every direction, for the scent
is all-pervasive. Into the empty lot, then, come the
rest of the dogs—collies and bulls, terriers and grey-
hounds, little Pekingese on tiny pads, St. Bernards
with tremendous paws, and mongrels of every size
and shape.

On the hillside above the field, I see alley cats
prowling nervously back and forth, watching me. And
from the edges of the field, peeking through the grass,
come numerous rats, mice, and moles. They've all
caught the scent. Humans can't perceive it, for their
noses have fallen into disuse. But we animals are inti-

mate with it, upon the vacant lot, as we gather in a sea of fangs and fur.

Naturally we look among us for leaders, for those dogs who might be able to interpret the subtleties of the scent and communicate more of it to us. And from the forest above the city, the wild dogs appear.

"Deceitful dog!"

We have several such dogs in the laboratory, stray mutts who are attempting to inflame our youth with revolutionary material. Naturally, we cut the dogs' vocal cords as soon as they enter the lab, but it's not enough, for as I'm sure you are aware, we animals have wordless communication, based on sensory impulses more subtle than language.

I've suggested to the Learned Professor time and again that we rats be given our own separate wing, but no. All the animals are here in one enormous room and we may have to pay dearly for it. Our current heatstroke study is utilizing a particularly rebellious mongrel dog, brought in from some alleyway, and he's filled with vicious propaganda. They have him chained to a treadmill inside a heated glass cage. He runs here, day in and day out, toward his death, which can come none too soon for me. I wish he'd drop dead from heat prostration this very moment, so I wouldn't have to listen to his twaddle.

He goes on night and day, sending us his inflammatory images. He's mute, but he's skillfully using the intuitive wavelength for his dastardly messages. I'm sure you can feel them in the air. His imagery is extremely fine and suggestive. A rat will be lying here, making a real contribution to science by having his trachea severed, and suddenly he'll be completely plugged into a revolutionary image. His whole body will be suffused with the feeling of freedom. Such feelings cannot be permitted, as you know.

"Good afternoon, Learned Professor!" Here comes

9

the Learned Pro again, but of course he doesn't acknowledge my greeting, for his intuitive wavelength is encrusted. It's a great pity because somehow I've got to get across to him the fact that he's got dangerous revolutionaries in his lab.

Oh my, here comes his lovely graduate assistant, her long blond hair curling softly around her shoulders. I'd certainly consider a copulation plug with her. Her ears would quiver as I stroked her on the neck, and after applying digital stimulation to her pelvis, you'd see a sudden curvature in her back, as she surrendered to my learned copulation-response test. Her superficial genitalia would appear in their characteristically blue color, matching her eyes, and she'd run around the wheel several times excitedly, then look at me apprehensively knowing that I, a vigorous white male, would attempt copulation seventy times in twenty minutes, with one or two ejaculations, ha ha!

I do hope I've got that right. Having been castrated at birth, I have no real firsthand knowledge of the matter. Naturally I keep my eyes and ears open here in the lab and I make careful field observations whenever a female begins stretching and bracing nervously. This blonde alongside the learned Professor is exhibiting every sign of entering her cycle of maximum sexual receptivity. She makes me feel dizzy, makes me start running around my turntable, round and round. It's a 12-inch metal disc (for more, see my learned paper, "Rats on the Wheel," *Psy. Journ.*, 1963). I've really got it clicking now. The cyclometer says I've already done fifteen revolutions!

That's enough to keep me in shape for a while. Now I must continue my rounds. Being a Learned Mad Professor, I've been given complete run of the maze table, which affords me points of contact with nearly every other section of the lab.

"Doctor Rat, I feel very strange."

"Certainly you do. Aren't you the rat who's being constantly crammed with wholly unsuitable food?"

"Yes, Doctor Rat, but this has nothing to do with that."

"What week of the diet are you in?"

"My fourth."

He has two weeks to go and then death will ensue, according to schedule. "I wouldn't worry about the way you feel, son. It's probably just the onset of keratinization of the corneal epithelium. You can't see straight is all."

"Doctor Rat, it's not a physical problem."

"They've had you in the maze, have they? Driven you slightly whacky, I imagine. Don't let it bother you. Once you go completely mad, you'll qualify for a degree in psychology."

"Doctor, it's not a mental problem either."

"Not physical and not mental? My boy, what else is there?"

"My spirit."

"Calcified kidneys and brittle bones, that's all that's troubling you, with maybe a little hyperirritability."

"No, Doctor, it's the very deepest part of me that I'm talking about."

"You mean deeper than a number eight French rubber catheter tude wth a depressed eye can go?"

"Deeper, much deeper."

"Are you trying to tell me, a Learned Mad Doctor, that there is some part of the rat as yet unknown to man?"

"My light, Doctor, the light inside me . . ."

". . . introduced through the rectum . . ."

"I saw a fountain of light inside me. Doctor, we come from that fountain."

"We come from the copulation plug, my lad. How old are you?" It's unfortunate that we don't have better sex education here in the laboratory. This is what comes of inserting glass rods into the vaginas of virgins.

"I'm ageless, Doctor, and timeless."

The poor overstuffed rat looks at me with such a gleam in his eyes that I'm certain he's being injected with small quantities of sodium amytal. There he goes, hobbling away to talk with the other rats, and spread his doctrine. I haven't got time for such things. Death is freedom, that's the all-inclusive doctrine.

The wild dogs, then, are our leaders. They say they've been on the scent for years, and it has led them here, to this great gathering of dogs. Now we'll move together, and move we do, out of the empty lot at the edge of town and into the forest, the wild dogs in the lead. Here they show their clear supremacy, going through the brush with paws that are swift and sure. They have the scent in their noses, and so do we. There are dogs on all sides, yapping through the trees and bushes.

Several old dogs are in our midst, their bellies fat and their eyes weak. Nonetheless they hold firm to the general movement. Those who abandon the march do so because the other scent—the scent of home—proves too strong for them.

I smell it, that old temptation. All of us, except the wild dogs, have to smell it because it's very strong, compounded of love, longing, and easy meals. We can smell it in the wind, we can smell it on the ground, we can smell it all around us and we run from it, knowing its danger. There are many heavy hearts though, and mine is one of them, for my masters are good and kind, thoughtful and gentle. . . .

But through the forest we plunge, putting the past behind us. We drink at little woodland streams, we sever our ties. And the stray dogs, who know the woods so well, race about us, inspiring us with their calls.

"Come on, dogs, come on!" they cry, and it's a wonderful, thrilling cry. The wild dogs are saturated with the mysterious scent, and inflamed by it—not mad, but rapturous, and their rapture is contagious. We run on, leaving love behind us.

In its place is a feeling of solidarity such as I forgot existed: to be with one's own, to follow one's own law, to hear the sound of one tongue speaking in the wind, with sunlight coming through the leaves, lighting the forest floor. I see a bright hallway of trees ahead of me, endless and beautiful. Out here, racing toward the sunset, my heart is my own and I'm free!

"Where are we bound for?" cry some of the doubtful dogs, their old homes still claiming them by a long leash.

"Just follow your nose, brother!" cries a laughing wild one, and away he leaps, with a fantastic spring in his legs. He's one of the intoxicated, so deep in the scent he seems to be flying along. The sight of his tail disappearing down the golden hallway sets me racing still faster, to catch him, to run with him at the very head of the pack. I exert myself to the fullest, enjoying my run. Without human eyes upon me, I'm unselfconscious. I'm myself, a dog in motion, howling and happy.

We follow that hallway of gold until it turns crimson, and still we run toward the setting sun. Now is the most beautiful running, with all figures blending into one, with all dogs looking the same, one mood upon us all. Where have I done this before? It seems so familiar—yet it's unlike anything I can remember from puppyhood on. But somewhere, sometime—in dreams, perhaps—I've run like this with my brothers, in the twilight of the day.

Feelings so pure and delicate assail my senses I can't restrain my barking. I yap, I howl, call to them all, saying, "Do you remember, do you remember?"

And "Yes!" they answer. "Yes, we remember!"

"What do you remember?"

"This, this!" they cry, as we run, down the wooded hillside, into the crimson valley, an open sky above our head.

We decide upon the valley as our lodging for the night. It's near water, and the sun is gone. We lie down and one by one the dogs at the rear of our run come into the valley and join us.

Exhausted, we speak little, wanting just to lie quiet for a while, as the stars slowly appear. Some of us bathe in the water, and some are still chasing around the edge of the pack exuberantly, but most of us lie still, tongues hanging out. The leaders take the center and form a single powerful unit, which we know must represent our will. And at the outer edge, too, there are strong watchers, seated and alert.

As I lie in the stillness, listening to the little brook beside me, the scent seems to be part of me. At the same time I know it's scattered like mist all around us. But that my own body is part of its chemistry, I can't deny.

"Where are we bound for?" ask some of the dogs again.

"Lie still, brothers," say the dogs of the center.

"What a smell, what a smell," says one old dog, limping out of the shadows. His hair is long and filled with burrs, and his eyes are watery. But he seems not to notice the bad shape he's in, so rapt is he in the wonder of the smell. "Always this smell," he says, lying down with the wild dogs. We see that he's forgotten his body, with all its old-dog woes. He's the first one to sleep and we see him twitch and run in his dreams, as if he were young again. He whimpers in the night, and he roars and when we wake in the morning he's dead and we eat him.

"Doctor Rat, Doctor Rat . . ."

A young female calling to me from her cage. She needs my special counseling, as she's all in a tizzy about the bandages on her belly. "Yes, my dear, are your bandages too tight?"

"They cut a hole in my stomach!"

"Yes, of course. It's so that they'll be able to insert a plastic window there in order to watch your embryonic ratlings develop."

"I hate it! I'll gnaw it off! I'll bite through the bandages!"

"Please, my dear, don't be hysterical." I must say she's not showing the scientific attitude at all. We've got to have that window there, so that we can insert a thin hair through it and tickle the little ratlings as they grow inside her. It's part of a new program, for which I'm preparing extensive notes. A great deal can be learned by tickling an embryo with a hair, but naturally only the most advanced graduate students are qualified for such tickling. How, then, can we expect this female rat to have any appreciation of the fine points of the Stomach-window Program? Nonetheless, it is my duty to make her more receptive to the learned hair.

"Please don't let them hurt me, please . . ."

I think a little song might cheer her up:

> *"Oh scaly skin and dandruff*
> *with hemorrhagic sores,*
> *come and look inside us,*
> *they've provided us with doors!"*

15

I must move along here to the next cage, where a special magnesium diet has caused fatal clonic convulsions:

> *"Oh loss of hair and nervousness,*
> *diarrhea too,*
> *goiter and spasticity*
> *combined with Asian flu!"*

"Doctor Rat, I can no longer eat!"

"Aren't you the lad whose teeth have been trained to grow into a complete circle, piercing the roof of the mouth?"

"A nightmare, Doctor Rat. My mouth's a nightmare."

"We're watching you with keen interest, my boy. There's a chance the teeth may actually grow right up and pierce your brain. Come along and sing with me! Sing:

> *Irregular ovulation and*
> *destruction of the thymus*
> *chronic lymphedema and*
> *amputation of the penis!"*

Excuse me, the Learned Professor has picked me up and is tying a string around my upper incisors at the moment. I am now permitted to hang by my teeth in the air as part of a new Insight Therapy Program —what fun, swinging back and forth here.

"Fight them, Doctor Rat! Bite them!"

A young radical rat shouting from his cage. Thus has our youth been corrupted by that goddamn blabber-mouth dog with his intuition-pictures. A rat may be waiting for decapitation, and suddenly he will see an intuitive play of pictures in his brain, sent there by this infernal dog on the treadmill. The rat will seem to participate in the scene, running with the wild dogs. The high intelligence of the dogs makes them very potent broadcasters, and being here under stress conditions adds power to their wavelength. Our lab is buzzing with revolutionary feelings. "You cock-sucking cur, how dare you sow dissent among these happy rats!"

The revolutionary mutt looks at me with red and squinting eyes. You perceived the subtlety of his broadcast, didn't you, with his sly insinuations of some sort of freedom to be gained by following a peculiar scent? But I know the truth and I'm shouting it to all: "The scent is five percent formaline, Brother Rats, and the only freedom you'll ever have is death! Death is freedom, that's the slogan!"

"Hurray for Doctor Rat!"

"You tell 'em, Doc."

"Thank you, friends and fellow supporters, thank you for your confidence. As you know, the rat is man's best friend. You've seen the advertisements in *Modern Psychology Magazine*: "The Rat Is Our Friend. Are we going to allow this wonderful friendship to go down the drain along with the cerebrospinal fluid? A rat must give his all! That's our purpose, that's why we're here on earth!"

My throat is certainly getting inflamed from all this. But I can't allow seventy-five years of laboratory experimentation to be pushed aside by a few revolutionary voices. This dog is in a powerful position, however, running here in our midst, tongue hanging out, legs flopping as the treadmill turns him, on and on. I've told the Learned Professor to jack up the heat in the dog's cage, so we can be finished with him soon. But the Learned Pro turns a deaf ear toward everything I say.

In the meantime, the dog has made numerous converts to his revolutionary cause. The whole Hemorrhagic Sore Cage has gone over to him. And I taught those ungrateful rats how to sing! What betrayal!

"Brother Rats, how can you be so easily swayed by this dirty dog? Look there, to your left. Look at the recipient rat on the surgical table. He's having a hole bored in his head. Listen to him screaming. The fresh tumor is being plunged into his brain tissue. In two or three weeks he'll be groveling around, the tumor increasing, obstructing all his bodily movements. That's reality, foolish rats. That's scientific reality, not a lot of stupid doggie drivel."

"Ah, go chase your tail, Doc. You're washed up around here!"

Those rats need to be shocked a few times down Maze Alleys A and D. They've lost all respect for my office. But I'm happy to see one of those rowdy rebel leaders being led to the cardiac puncture table. He's struggling, his teeth showing white and vicious.

"Fellow rat, now that your supreme scientific moment has come, don't you want to have a change of heart? Give your all to science happily. Set an example for these other young rats."

Several revolutionaries quickly move in front of me. "Don't say another word, Rat. Don't mock him in his agony."

"Mocking? Who's mocking? I'm here to eulogize the fellow, to write him up in glowing terms in the Newsletter. If you'll permit me to pass . . ."

The rebels block the way. The Learned Professor is feeling the rat's chest for the point of maximum palpitation. There, he's got it now, his thumb and forefinger on the fourth, fifth, and sixth ribs.

Now comes the needle, 26-gauge, half an inch long. The plunger is grasped and the needle is pushed slowly into the rat's heart. The Learned Pro will be withdrawing about 10 cc's of blood and that should finish this rebel off.

Good heavens! The blood is squirting right out of the rat's heart into the Learned Professor's eye! The Learned Pro is looking around puzzled as the blood drips down his cheek. I certainly won't be able to use this item in my Newsletter.

Everywhere around me—little accidents, little problems. It's the effect of the revolutionary dogs, and I fear it's going to spread like wildfire.

My front paws are tied, but my rear legs are free on the treadmill and forced to run, to go nowhere inside a glass cage. My tongue is hanging out, my body weary. The men have heated the glass cage I'm in, so that it seems I'm running beneath the blazing sun, on and on, going nowhere.

I've been on this treadmill all week, and still I'm running, on and on, saliva dripping heavily from my mouth, mixed with bitter bile. The men stand and watch me as I run. I'm caught here, tied and heated, choking with thirst, my body soaked with sweat, my insides churning with pain. Hot like a desert, on and on I run . . .

. . . run . . . run . . . run . . . run . . . run as the wheel keeps turning, keeps clicking. Bright hot coils surround me on all sides, baking me, my cage an oven.

Run. Tongue out, dry and cracked. Run. Legs burning, my skin blistering, I retch up my bilious guts.

Run . . . run . . . run . . . run . . . run. Run, dogs, run. Run through the day . . . run through the night . . . run through the endless desert heat . . . heat without water . . . wheel without end . . . my eyes are on fire, my tongue is swollen, my throat is bubbling.

Run, dogs, run! Free yourselves! Run out into the sun. We're meeting at the edge of town. See us circling there. Join us there! Come, dogs, come!

"Oh, you disgusting dog! Go back to the alleyway you came from and stop shaming the good citizens of this laboratory with your perverted view of life!"

I think I've finally gotten through to the Learned Professor. He turned up the heat in the dog's cage this morning. The dog's skin is cracking with blisters and his mouth is foaming. He'll soon drop. But the Learned P. has twenty-five more dogs standing by to take their turn on the treadmill. And every one of them is a potential revolutionary! "What have you dogs got to complain about! You get your bowl of fox chow every morning, don't you? What could be nicer than that?"

They just stare at their leader, watching him as he flops along, his legs slapping up and down as the treadmill turns beneath him. Can you see the cloud of forms emanating from him? His revolutionary program billows and drifts all over our laboratory, infiltrating its way into every cage. See it there—dogs floating in the air, in full command of the intuitive band. They've taken over the central station. Their broadcast is reaching into the minds and hearts of every animal foolish enough to tune in. The noble function of intuition, through which the age-old secrets of our race are transmitted, is now in the hands of a revolutionary gang of mutts.

"I implore you, fellow rats and fellow animals everywhere—turn to another channel! We're running a film strip today on mechanical injuries to the teeth of canines. It's very informative, you'll see how to fracture

a hound's tooth and bring about some marvelous hypo-
plastic defects. These will result in slowing the growth
of all the other teeth in a dog, and I say that's a good
thing! Dogs have too many teeth. They're vicious and
dangerous and . . ."

It's so hard to get their interest. The dog's program is more subtly suggestive. It works on the weak-
ness of my fellow rats. They don't realize that we're
the friends of man, that we're here to serve humanity
selflessly in every way we can. For only in man does
one find the divine spark. The rest of us live in darkness, without souls.

"You're all just basic models, fellow rats! Don't
you understand the meaning of that? A basic model
has no feelings, has no spirit. Man is able to twist us
and starve us and cut off our tails because that's the
law! Haven't you read St. Thomas Aquinas? Animals
have no soul!"

I'm growing hoarse trying to get the truth across
to the Experimental Radiation Cage. All the rats in
there have clubbed paws and absent toes and you'd
think they'd be able to listen to reason. But no—they're
sitting there, staring into space, entranced by the dog's
broadcast.

"Five percent formaline, that's the scent! Believe
me, fellow rats, there is no magic scent in the air. Look
there—the dog has collapsed on the treadmill, his legs
flopping lifelessly. He's dead! Look at the eyes rolled
into his head and his body thumping along. He's dead!
And death is the only freedom!"

The Learned Professor and his graduate assistants
have opened the dog's cage and are taking him away.
His body is thin and dehydrated, but his infernal
message goes on!

"Plug your ears, rats. Don't listen!"

The Learned Prof is leading another dog into the
glass chamber, tying his front paws to the rack. Now
the power is switched on again and the treadmill is
turning once more and another martyr is being created!
Professor, I beg of you, get those dogs out of here!

He doesn't hear me. Professor, you're playing

right into their hands! Don't let him run along in sight of all the other animals. Because the fumes of revolution are rising out of him already. Can't you see!

No, the L.P. doesn't see the powerful images pouring forth from that damned dog. But we can! We see dogs of all kinds, leaving their homes, leaving their posts, running away. They run in the air all around us as the intuitive picture grows brighter. The dog has conjured up trees and dusty roads and sparkling streams. A terrible power is at work in our laboratory, obliterating the wire cages and the operating tables and the exercise wheels. All of the marvelous equipment is being submerged behind a woodland scene.

"Don't look, fellow rats, don't look! Concentrate instead on the Shock Discrimination Box. Look at your fellow rats in there, jumping in the air after touching the electric grid. They're being driven slowly insane. They're going to receive their Mad Doctor's diploma soon. Isn't that worth working for? Chronically disordered behavior isn't something we get for nothing, just because we're rats. We have to earn our neurosis. Come over here and join in with those rats being tormented by the Disturbing Bell Stimuli. You know how sensitive our ears are; they're the perfect instrument for mankind to work with. I'd like you to observe carefully now—that's it, don't look at the disgusting doggie broadcast—observe how your fellow rat is being skillfully used. A bell is being rung alongside his head while his cage is oscillated in the air in an arc of 180 degrees. It's enough to make anybody feel strange, wouldn't you say? Swinging back and forth, with bells ringing all around you, you start to feel tense and frightened. Look, look, look at how the bell is being brought nearer, then moved away, now near again, threatening and retreating once more. Now, now! There, the rat has gone into a seizure, running around his cage and bumping into the walls. Look at him rolling over on his side with his legs kicking in the air. His body is trembling, and he has ticlike movements of the head. He's a candidate for a Mad Doctor's degree! Congratulations, my boy! We'll be throwing a pressed biscuit banquet in your honor a little later on!"

Well, now, here's a distinct improvement: The Learned Professor is bringing out his cigarette lighter. I hadn't thought we'd be doing this experiment again, but of course we've got to repeat these experiments in order to validate our findings.

The graduate assistant has selected a floppy-eared cocker spaniel for the experiment. Another assistant ties down the cocker's paws. Excellent, very smooth work. You young folks are Doctor Rat's pride and joy.

The nice doggie-woggie is all strapped down. And he won't be doing much revolutionary broadcasting, I guarantee.

The Learned Professor is flicking his lighter—he's got it lit—now he adjusts it so that it shoots out a long tongue of flame.

Doggie-woggie is looking at the flame, now looking at the Professor. Oh, you'll like this one, Doggie!

The Learned Professor brings the flame right into the dog's nostril, shoots it right up there. Excellent, well-aimed. The cocker is being forced to *inhale the flame*. Now the assistant lights his own lighter and both nostrils are filled with fire, as the dog's mouth snaps open in a soundless howl.

I'm sorry to say that this experiment is not original with our great university. It was dreamed up at Harvard. Well, of course Harvard's one of the better schools, and I'm not really jealous. Hand in hand with Harvard, we're continuing the great Burning Issue Experiment. It's essential, it's informative, it's good for the nation.

That's it, Doggie, take a good deep noseful of fire. You'll like it.

This is the sort of experiment that doesn't cause much trouble. The dog is too panicked to send out any revolutionary signals. I wish I could say the same for our Pain Threshold Experiment over in the corner. It's not going well at all, because it proceeds at a slow, steady pace. Anything that lingers that way gives the dog a chance to concentrate, to produce the revolutionary signal.

Shall we look at the experiment more closely?

One of our graduate assistants has been working for the past hour. He has a rawhide mallet. Watch closely now: The assistant raises the mallet and whacks the dog in the leg with it. Another assistant keeps count. That's blow number 573. The dog will receive exactly a thousand blows on the leg, which is the number that Columbia University has established as necessary to produce shock. We're indebted to the Learned Pros of Columbia for this information.

We lift our heads and howl, and the wild dogs lead us onward. Through the forest we race once again, with the dew upon us. The variety of smells is wonderfully sweet. How did I ever forsake this for a life of captivity, a life of subservience? I sold my soul for comfort, for security, for a leash. But there are others less eager than I.

"This is folly. Our masters are calling us!"

"Rid yourself of illusions!" cries a wild dog, leaping like a streak of light and then going far ahead.

We emerge from the forest onto a dirt road and run down it, in the warm summer air. It's a small and winding road, leading through farmland. Ahead of us, floating on the air, is the scent of man. We surge forward, afraid of nothing. Our numbers are great now, and we run on over the hill, catching sight of the man below. He's working with a horse who pulls a fallen tree along the road.

The man hears our howling and turns toward us. Seeing the torrent of teeth and tails he turns and runs into the forest. The work horse, still dragging his log, tries to follow the man, but the log catches in a tangle of smaller trees and the horse can't move. We see his trembling muscles and his frightened eyes.

"Come with us!" we cry. "Can't you smell what's in the air?"

The horse struggles to follow his master. If the wonderful smell has reached him, he gives no sign of it. He's securely in the traces, he's forgotten his nature. Realizing he's lost, we race past him then and on up the road, with the warm dust beneath our paws and the smell inside our nose.

25

"Pure bile, fellow rats, that's what this talk of freedom is, pure green bile. It's a result of an infection in the dog's liver, that's all."

Things have gone from bad to worse here in the lab. My fellow rats are deserting the ship of science in great numbers. They're snapping and biting at the graduate assistants, and the Learned Professor has begun mass innoculations against parasitic flukes of the Echinostomatidae family. But it's the dog family that's troubling our guts, Professor, not the flukes. I would much prefer microscopic worms in my intestines to these blasted dogs in my eardrums with their slobbering tale of freedom. Please, Professor, get them out of here!

They've hooked up their signal to the signal coming out of Creighton University. You recall the Creighton Starvation Experiment. A group of dogs was starved for sixty-five days. The important information resulting from this experiment did not surface immediately, I regret to say, as our learned Creighton colleagues preferred to be secretive about their work in order not to have anybody steal the march on them. They were so secretive that a different group of young Creighton scientists *duplicated* the experiment three years later.

It was this repetition of the starvation experiment that caused a definite signal to emanate from Creighton U's campus. Anyone on the intuitive band can see it hovering outside the Creighton lab—a sort of faint, fading photograph of emaciated dogs, their ribs sticking out, their eyes sunk deep in their heads. This inspiring photograph, which should have become a hallowed bit of scientific testimony, has instead been picked up by the rebels. They're using it as their channel pattern-picture. Any animal who started to drift off onto the intuitive band around three o'clock in the morning, when nothing else is on the tube, sees that photo, accompanied by a long, low howl. It's this revolutionary use of our priceless scientific film strips that I find so disgusting. The young Creighton professors worked long and hard starving those dogs.

You rebels have stolen our studies! You've copped the bones! And you won't get away with it, I promise you. You'll all be inhaling flames, dear rebels. Harvard will make sure of it.

And the good professors of Columbia will club the shit out of you, first chance they get!

How convenient that reprisals and punishment can be part of further learning programs. While those rebels are being burned and beaten for their revolutionary activity, our young students will be taking careful notes and making snapshots for the yearbook. Everything will turn out right in the end—if we squash the rebels now!

But unfortunately the rebel network is enlarging. If you'll cast your eyes over to that work table, you'll see what I mean.

No, no, I don't mean that lovely young blond assistant. Yes, she'd probably throw a good copulation plug, but I mean to draw your attention to the *egg* she's holding in her hand.

It's just an ordinary fertilized egg, and our lovely blondie is only going to do some research into embryonic development. But—in these inflamed times every lower-life form is radiating an intense signal on extrasensorial TV.

Do you see what I mean? The egg is broadcasting!

We live in eternal day. It makes us lay more. We live on wire flooring so that our excrement will fall through onto the constantly turning belt below, which carries it away. Our beaks have been cut off. And we're cancerous. They call us egg machines.

We're the best egg machines in the world. Twenty-seven thousand of us sit here, our only exercise the laying of an egg, which rolls away from us, down a little chute.

I remember how wonderful it was to peck my way through the shell and step out into the warm bright dawn of life.

I have seen no other sunrise. We live in eternal noontime. My birth was a grievous mistake. And yet an egg is developing in me, as always. I can't stop it. I feel its growth, and despite all my bitterness, tiny surges of tenderness fill me. How I wish I could stop the egg from growing so that I wouldn't have to know these tender feelings. But I can't stop. I'm an egg machine, the best egg machine in the world.

"Don't be so gloomy, Sister. There are better times coming."

The insane hen in the cage beside mine has fallen victim to a common delusion here at the egg factory. "No better times are coming, Sister," I reply. "Only worse times."

"You're mistaken, my dear. I happen to know. Very soon we'll be scratching in a lovely yard."

I don't bother to reply. She's cheered by her delusions. And since our end will be the same, what does it matter how we spend our days here? Let her dream in her lovely yard. Let her develop her dream to its fullest, until she imagines that the wire floor beneath her claws has become warm dry earth. We don't have much longer to go. Our life span is only fourteen months of egg laying and then we're through.

An egg machine!

There's a great fluttering of wings along this cell block, and much loud clucking. The cages are opening, and one by one rough hands grab us.

"You see, Sister. I told you better times were coming. Now we'll be going out into the lovely yard."

"Yes, Sister. Now we're finally going."

Now we're hung upside down, our feet tied together with wire.

"You see, Sister. It's just as I told you—the better times have come at last."

We're hooked to a slowly moving belt. Hanging upside down, we're carried along through a dark tunnel. The wire bites into my flesh. Swaying through the darkness we go. The gurgling cries up ahead of us make clear what better times have come.

"Our reward, Sister, is here at last," cries our mad sister. "We were good and laid many eggs and now we get our reward."

The cry of each hen is cut off so that her squawking becomes liquid bubbling. And then the sound of dripping: drip, drip, drip.

"Oh, I can see it now, Sister, the lovely yard I spoke of, all covered with red flowers and . . ."

The mash runs out of her neck.

"Chicken manure, fellow rats, believe me, that's all this talk is."

But look how it has excited the colony. Teeth bared, tails twitching, eyes blazing, the whole laboratory is in rebellion. I searched the files and couldn't find a single thing like it anywhere, and I went all the way back to the early work of Doctor Claude Bernard in Paris in 1876. You recall Doctor Bernard's immortal words to his students: "Why think when you can experiment?"

I admit quite humbly to having received the Claude Bernard Animal Experimentation Award the year I went mad, so I'm familiar with every possible kind of laboratory situation, and there's nothing like this present rebellion in any of the records.

Oh, for the good old days when our conflict-situations were all experimentally produced.

Now a bunch of armchair lawyers from the Protein Deficiency Cage have joined the incendiary campaign, trying to convince the little ratlings that they have certain rights.

"Don't listen to these albino assholes, my little ratlings. Listen to your true friend, the good Doctor Rat, and learn about gut reality (see my paper, "Removal of the Rat's Stomach," *Anat. Dig.,* 1967). I wouldn't steer you wrong, you know that. Let's all do the little dance called the New Necropsy! Come on, ratlings, dance with Doctor Rat, and sing:

Do the New Necropsy
Let me see you quiver and quake!

Do the New Necropsy
when they extirpate your liver and take
your head off with a cleaver
do the New Necropsy and shake, shake, shake!"

"Be quiet, Doctor Rat. We're listening to the dog."

"That dog is full of shit, my friends. Look at the way his feces are streaked. Look at his heaving sides and belly. He's an enemy of the state!"

I slink away, exhausted. Interpretive dancing is not my forte, but I would do anything to save my beloved laboratory. Oh, for the good old days when we all used to sit around the cisternal puncture stand and sing harmoniously about having our frontal lobes removed. Those were dear sweet times. I miss them terribly. I feel so alienated.

". . . when a chicken's neck is wrung, the following should be done: Hold the bird by the head, placing the fingers just behind the skull. Then force the right hand down. The neck is thus elongated. At the same time, turn the bird's head backward, bending it over the neck. This will dislocate the neck . . ."

"Oh, be quiet, you stupid egg!" What do I, a Learned Mad Doctor, care how a chicken's neck is wrung?

I have important papers to write. I have to mount a counteroffensive against these dogs and that half-cracked egg. But I just don't have my usual zip. One of my favorite experiments, the 500-pound pressure clamp, is taking place right now, and it's not giving me the kick it used to, because I know the rebels will try to make propaganda out of it.

And what could be more innocent than this— come on, step over here behind me and see for yourself. There's a big, stupid-looking spotted dog, right? Alongside him a graduate assistant.

The graduate ass. is making a very delicate appraisal of the experimental situation. One day his findings will be published in a little-known scientific journal and earn him a degree. But that won't be the end of this intrepid work. Not at all. It will eventually become part of a complete textbook on the subject.

He'll be able to hold his head up high in the hallway. He'll get a raise in pay. Why?

Because he is presently turning the screw attached to that dog's leg. The pressure is being raised in proportion to the desired raise in pay. The higher the pressure applied to this dog's leg, the higher will the young man's salary go. The gauge indicates that the pressure is now at 250 pounds.

You'll have to do better than that, young fellow, if you want the Dean of Science to give you his blessing. Your predecessors in this department had the pressure up to 500 pounds last year. Go ahead, pour it on! Make that dog really jump. Crush his bones to mush and your M.A. is assured.

The logic of this Pressure Program is irrefutable. It keeps our university filled with valuable grants. It's good for the economy and it's good for humanity. This dog's crushed leg will serve as a guideline for future studies of a similar nature, which will ultimately culminate in a magnificent scientific breakthrough of the bones.

It might also result in a better kind of plastic, or perhaps a new sort of aspirin. Housing projects will be more perfectly designed and detergents will improve. The applications are simply endless.

But the rebels are making hay with it!

The fuckers.

Distorting it all out of proportion. Making it seem cruel. What's cruel about crushing a dog?

A dog is just a basic model. A convenient evolutionary offshoot expressly designed for the laboratory.

"We're going to recruit the dogs of this village," say the wild leaders.

And so we wait, remaining on the dirt road. Ahead, the dirt turns into pavement, and a few old houses stand there, deserted. But far below, in the valley, we can see the other houses of the village, and there are people there, people—and dogs.

Here comes a bloodhound, hot on the scent. His big nose travels on the ground, and he keeps shaking his head, unable to detect exactly where the smell is, whether in the gutter or in the sky. His big ears droop along, almost touching the ground and his short legs carry him slowly forward, until he sees us, massed ahead of him—a sea of eyes and noses and tails and teeth.

He sits back on his hind legs and peers cautiously toward us, his nose in the air, sniffing furiously.

"Come on, come on," we cry.

Hearing the friendly barking, and trusting in the wonderful smell, he comes forward. I can see the look in his eyes. He has a name, this bloodhound, and his name is still important to him. Were his master to cry out, "Here, Blacky," or "Here, Spot," he would turn and answer. But we draw him into our ranks, get him deep in the middle where our burning soul will envelop his name and destroy it forever. Still his eyes are filled with apprehension. He wants to be free to follow the scent, yet his old personality pulls him back.

"This is just a pack," he says. "I don't want to be just part of a pack."

"Pack?" cries a wild dog. "There is no pack!"

A shudder runs through me, as if I'm caught on the end of a line connected to a distant star and that star is drawing me, out of my body, out and out. I spin toward the wild dog; his eyes blaze into mine, flaming like stars set deep in the endless sky, made of brilliant light, increasing in brilliance until his whole body is shining.

Terrified, I spin away from him, only to see that all the dogs are shining that way, that indeed there are no dogs, there is only one vast shining body, the Dog Star.

Sweet Jumping Dormice! (family *Zapodidae*)

A group of rebel rat mothers are marching around on the exercise wheel, shouting slogans. Their leaders are a pair of rats who were stitched together last week. It was a lovely and important parabiosis. Their skin was slit from head to tail and their flesh joined together, along with their clavicle bones and abdominal muscles (see my paper "Parabiotic Rats," *Exper. Biol.,* 1972). Such contributions to science are incalculable in their benefits to mankind. How can these rats be so selfish! Just because we haven't yet determined the deep significance of stitching two rats together does not mean we won't eventually find out. We'll keep on stitching! "Close your ears, fellow rats! Don't listen to these irresponsible rabble rousers. Remember that you are contributing to research, to saving the lives of millions of human beings. . . ."

"Please look at my newborn ratlings, Doctor. Look at them playing and frisking about. Why should their lives be ruined by horrible diets and terrible surgery?"

"BECAUSE GOD WANTED IT THAT WAY, YOU RIDICULOUS PAIR OF STITCHED-TO-GETHER RAT BASTARDS!"

Oh my, I'm getting quite upset by all this. It isn't proper for a Learned Mad Doctor to shout from the cage tops this way. I'd better go over here and continue my note taking on the heatstroke study, in a manner more befitting a scientist of my stature.

I see they've got the water boiling. Shall we listen to the Learned Professor and his retinue? It will do your heart good, I think. I know it always makes me feel secure when I hear them talking this way:

"Temperature should be 140 degrees."

"We're ready with it, Professor."

As you can see, the basic model in this experiment is a rabbit. He's wearing a rather ingenious bathing cap. It's actually a double bonnet, watertight, fitted snugly to the rabbit's head.

The graduate assistant is now pouring—there it goes—the boiling water into the rabbit's bonnet. Look at that big-footed fucker kick! (*Lepus americanus*) His eyes are bulging out and his breathing grows rapid as the bonnet is filled to capacity with the boiling water. The water is scalding his whole noggin. Isn't this exciting?

I have observed that a very definite sexual tension is produced in the laboratory whenever such dramatic experiments take place. The Learned Professor and his staff are gripped by such tension now. It's a very delicate undercurrent which only a specialist like myself can detect. But I've nibbled a few pages of Sigmund Freud in my spare time, and it's quite clear that such experiments are definite outlets for sexual energy. I may prepare a little paper on this subject, to be privately circulated. But let's listen to our students:

"His eyes are sensitive to the touch, Professor."

"Yes, that's as it should be. Bring on the hotter water now."

"We're ready with it, sir. It's 180 degrees."

The bonnet is drained of the first flood of hot water and now they're pouring in still hotter. Wow, look at that rabbit squirm! Take note how his stomach bulges and contracts spasmodically. This is the heart and soul of our work. His eyes are rolling in his head.

"All right, don't waste any time!"

The rabbit has stiffened and gone still. But the students are only beginning their important probe. The bonnet is removed and a surgical cut is made in the skull. A thermometer is placed inside the brain. A grad holds it there, and all watch him with unflinching attention. Slowly he draws it out of the rabbit's skull and wipes off the brain fluid. Now he's looking at it, and now:

"117 degrees Fahrenheit."

"That's just about right. Have you got the next model ready?"

"We'll be running it on two cats, Professor. Then we thought we'd try it on a kitten."

"Good. You fellows should take a break first. Co-ordinate your notes. And one of you can heat up the oven."

"Yes sir."

The Learned Professor leaves the lab. His students go to the coffee machine. They don't notice an escaped rebel rat hiding under the percolator. No, and they don't smell him either, as he drops a turd in their paper cup. The graduate assistants are turning on the radio, taking a break, not suspecting what's going on under their noses.

". . . on *Information Radio this afternoon, we have sunny skies—and quite a long list of runaway dogs. Must be spring in the air, folks! If you see a black, brown, and white female beagle, named Daisy, four years old . . .*"

Great Naked Mole Rats! This is terrible! The dogs are rebelling *outside* the laboratory too!

". . . *small hound, black and white, answers to the name of Sarge . . .*"

To the name of *Revolutionary*, you mean! What a shock. This is worse than Maze Alley D!

". . . *a black spaniel, named Pepsi . . .*"

Now, dogs, through this stream. We race across the water, barking, splashing, wildly excited. We have the farm dogs and the city dogs and all the lone-wolf dogs. I feel the ancient doghood in me rising, as the pride of my race is recovered from its long burial. My view was limited; I thought that humans were wiser than I.

We are the wise and the brave. Now my heart regains itself. We have wisdom when we have this unity. It plays among us as we run with our own kind. How deep is the dog's spirit, how deep and free!

Dance, dogs, dance! The race has been freed from its delusion.

Long ago we crept toward the fires of men, not knowing what subservience lay hidden there for us. Man isn't ruler.

There are no rulers!

There is only the streaming I feel now, here, as the well-springs of our spirit erupt.

There are no masters!

How cleverly men have deceived us, making us think they were wise. Cunning, yes, they're cunning as coyotes, but wisdom is found only here, in the streaming, in the freedom, in the gathering of our hearts as one.

Through the leaves, then, and down the long-lost paths of adventure. I licked their hands for a cracker, for whatever they tossed me, but now—now I lick the forest stream as cold as the morning and clear.

If I starve, I don't care. If I die, it'll be here, in my only domain, the high green hills, the low rolling val-

leys, beneath the desolate tree. I piss where I please, we
piss in the air, we race as we want to, without someone waiting with a leash.

A leash!

Caught by the neck! How horrible, what impossible confinement I've suffered—but never, ever again.
Men love leashes. They all wear them, I've learned.
Tying leashes on each other, keeping each other
bound.

We tunnel through the branches and leap into the
wet swamp grass. Then, exhausted, we rest, here by the
edge of the swamp, upon the soft moss.

I thought somehow, when I was a slave, that the
deep sweet moments I occasionally had were some sort
of gift from the wind, bestowed now and then, but
never for long. And I would look up at my master and
lick his hand in confusion, thinking that he knew all
the deep sweet gifts of the day, that he had mastered
those gifts, possessed them utterly.

What a fool I was.

Man has none of them! I know this for certain;
it's unmistakably clear. His habits are obvious to me
now, how dry and unfulfilled he is, how he sought
fulfillment in me!

I lie here, breathing the sublime odors of the
forest, and the deep sweet moment is mine constantly.
Oh, how wise the wild dogs were, to have known this
and never surrendered.

We need nothing from men.

They, in constrast, need something from us. They
desperately need to run this way, through the forest,
with nose to the ground. But they never will. They're
leashed to a doorstep, chained on the lawn.

The dogs around me all see it now. Their dark
eyes are sparkling with our realization, their tails are
wagging happily. The spaniel rolls over, kicking his
feet in the air. Here, in the wilderness, in the dense dark
abode of the dog, the dog comes to himself, after sleeping so long in a chair.

These rebels broadcasts are so unnerving, and here I am trying to make out my monthly Public Health Report on our high-frequency heat radiation experiment in cage 7. It's part of an important series of experiments begun in 1926. Thanks to a powerfully glowing vacuum tube, we've already scorched the fur off several of the caged rats.

"My paws . . . all burned . . ."

"I can't . . . breathe . . ."

As you can hear for yourself, these results conform exactly to those gotten for the past forty-eight years (see my paper, "On Roasting a Rat," *Journ. Med.*, 1970). Only through such careful comparisons can we be assured that there will be enough grants to go around next year. Giving unstintingly of their time and effort, my colleagues, etc. . . . I know how to phrase these reports. The trained scientific writer is able to present a thorough and completely obscure summary of his findings. No one will contradict the Learned Professor because nobody knows exactly what he's doing, or why. It is sufficient that each month we mention cancer and a new kind of plastic.

However, my report is not complete until I include the present microwave-oven experiment. Here comes the assistant now, carrying a tray of kittens. How cute they are, with their paws taped down onto the tray. How sweet and lovable and unable to move. The door is opened in the oven, and now, as you can see, the kittens, fully awake, are being placed into the heated chamber.

"175 degrees . . ."

Watch this, the tails will actually sizzle and explode.

". . . vaginal bleeding . . ."

Right, *vaginal bleeding,* I'm taking it all down in shorthand.

"Note how the extremities turn blue. . . . We should have interesting brain cell damage. . . ."

Brain cell damage, got it.

"Very alert, aren't they?"

"The Yale experiments in '54 had only ordinary ovens . . . but they still produced significant cell damage in the cerebellum and frontal lobes. . . ."

This is the sort of gratifying sight the taxpayers don't usually have a chance to see—two young scientists in front of the oven, baking a trayful of cats. This is where your taxes are going, fellow Americans, contributing to a better and lasting etcetera.

". . . Rochester University . . . 1969 . . ."

". . . microwave damage indistinguishable from fever in general . . ."

All right, I think that should do nicely, fellows. The Public Health officials will be impressed by your brain cell damage, and I myself am quite pleased to see that whole tray of dead kitties.

"NO MORE ANIMAL EXPERIMENTATION!"

"We want our rights!"

Oh my goodness, the rebel rats are screaming from their cages! How unseemly. I'm only glad that our two young cat-baking graduates aren't able to detect these intuitive signals. It would interfere with their concentration, and they have important dissection to perform now on the dead kittens. I'll have to deal with these rowdy rebels:

"Please, my dear fellow rats, your demands are simply outrageous. Restrain your tails in a turkish towel, folded along the line C-D (Fig. 19) and fasten them with safety pins ("Restraining the Rat," *Mag. Psych. Gen.,* 1965)."

Fortunately, there's only one more experiment left on the schedule for today. Let me see . . . yes . . . carbon monoxide . . . very good.

Please step over here to the glass enclosure. It's the perfect size for a beagle hound, isn't it. And here comes the dumb mutt now, his ears flopping as he's led toward the enclosure. I'm actually very fond of dogs, in their place.

Come on, Doggie, just step this way. Don't worry about this strange-looking glass room. It's just a shower bath. Yes, that's right, we're just going to give you a little shower and get rid of your fleas. Lots of nice beagles have taken this shower bath, that's a good doggie, step right through the door.

The beagle is safely enclosed inside the shower room. And now the graduate assistant starts up the small gasoline motor which exhausts itself into the glass cage. The beagle looks around nervously, and now his long nose is twitching in the air as he smells the exhaust. Sing:

> "How much is that doggie in the window,
> the one with the long floppy ears . . ."

He paws at the glass, peering out at us, panic in his eyes. The graduate assistants, I'm happy to say, remain calm and clinically alert. They aren't taken in by that hang-dog look, as the beagle flops on the floor of the shower room, unable to stand. Do you like your nice shower, Doggie? You won't have to scratch those nasty fleas anymore.

"Are you timing it?"

"Yes, I've got it marked down."

Very good, students, timing is essential. Not every dog dies quite the same way in this chamber. Some are more resistant than others. If we could understand those differences in resistance to the deadly fumes, we might succeed in producing a better shoe polish for the army. Of course, it will require a great many more beagles, but we've got them, my friends, and the Pentagon's got the funds. You two students can look forward to at least three years' research right here at the shower baths.

The dog is crawling weakly around the glass, his eyes clouded over. Look—he wagged his tail!

Well, now, there—his tongue has flopped out and he's rolling over on his side. A last twitch of his hind leg, and—his shower is over. That didn't take too long, did it? What a good stiff doggie.

Take him right to the incinerator, boys. We won't need any dissecting of the corpse. The timing is the important factor. That's it, just wrap him in a newspaper. The university incinerator is plenty big enough to handle him. This potential enemy of the state has yielded an important piece of scientific evidence, and soon he'll be a little curl of smoke in the air, blowing over the campus. Do you see, rebellious animals—the only way you'll ever escape from here is out the chimney, ha ha!

A long hard day at the lab. The grads and the Learned Professor are removing their white coats and hanging them up in the corner. Don't worry, gentlemen, the faithful Doctor Rat will watch over the lab for you during the night. I won't let these rebels get away with any funny business.

See you tomorrow.

Lights out, door closing, *click.*

I guess I'll go over to the bookshelf and do a little light nibbling. A Learned Mad Doctor has got to keep up with the latest texts on who drove whom whacky and how.

What's that shadow I see slipping along the shelf?

An escaped rebel rat! He's racing along toward the laboratory radio. Wrapping his tail around the knob, he switches it on!

"*. . . authorities continue to be concerned by the growing number of dogs that have gathered together at the outskirts of the city. Unconfirmed reports from other parts of the state have indicated that the phenomenon may be widespread. State and local police are now on the alert for packs of . . .*"

I slept in the cave of the ancients. I lay hidden in the secret den. I arose and left my cave, for my sleep was troubled. And the wind carried me. I blew over the land, gathering the scattered limbs of my body. Now I am He of a Million Eyes. Now I have many teeth and many tails. Now run, dogs, run! Run with me, to the City of Blood, where Death does his long-dying dance!

I am a howling river, a torrent of raging power. I am the Ancient Dog, He of a Million Tails. Through the meadows I rush, and through the broken lanes of the forest. The City of Blood lies not far ahead. I know the way, for its smell has long troubled my sleep and its cries have ruined my dreams.

Their crying brought me awake. Astonished, I saw them being bred by men for their flesh, being herded and tortured, imprisoned and maimed. They cry out from the moment of birth to the hour of death, and their crying has brought me awake. It cannot go on this way. The law has been violated. We are all one creature, except for man, who refuses to recognize himself in our eyes. I, the Lord of Animals, protest!

I have taken the form of the dog, friend of man. I am the beagle and the Doberman, the spaniel and the terrier, the collie and the setter, the greyhound and the wild dog, the stray dog and the old dog, the ruined and the wise dog, the timid and the fierce dog. I run to the edge of the City of Blood.

I am the shadow upon the hill. My million red eyes stare down.

"What a pile of dog shit this is, my fellow rats! Don't let these fragmentary delusions of grandeur provoke you...."

It's that damned dog in the pressure clamp. Do you see the fearful image he's sending out on the intuitive band? "Go on, get back in your basket, you Pomeranian piss pot!"

Fortunately, these intuitive signals have no basis in reality. They're loose hypnogogic fantasies; a few stray dogs, perhaps, have gotten together and are making a lot of noise in an alley somewhere, and these rebels are trying to blow it up into something great and grand.

But a Learned Mad Doctor isn't taken in so easily. Recall: the memoirs of Michael Mus Musculus, the lunatic mouse who believed he'd created the world out of his excrement.

So ignoring these paranoids, let's just slip out of Maze Alley D, and go along here to the laboratory library. Curl your tail up and let's continue reading this Johns Hopkins University research report. Valuable, authenticated material, not some Pekingese pipe dream. Now, Johns Hopkins, let's hear what your students have been doing:

> We pinched their tails, their feet, and their ears. We picked them up by the loose skin of the back and shook them. We spanked them and determined their response to restraint . . . quite intense and prolonged nociceptive stimuli were applied. . . . Such procedures as tying her in the dorsal decubitus on an animal board, picking her up by the loose skin of the back, and vigorously shaking

45

*her, spanking her, or pinching her tail as hard as
possible between thumb and forefinger elicited
only a few plaintive meows. When her tail was
grasped between the jaws of a large surgical
clamp and compressed sufficiently to produce a
bruise she cried loudly and attempted to escape
. . . during the 139 days of survival she was subjected, every two or three days, to a variety of
noxious stimuli . . . on one occasion her tail,
shaved and moistened, was stimulated tetanically
through electrodes connected with the secondary
of a Harvard inductorium, the primary circuit of
which was activated by 4.5 volts. When the secondary coil was at 13, she mewed; at 11 there was
loud crying . . . at the end of the 5-second stimulation with the secondary at 5 she screamed loudly and spat twice. The last of these stimulations
produced a third-degree electrical burn of the tail.*

Brilliant! What intelligence use of a cat. These
Johns Hopkins boys are way ahead of the field. I must
show this material to my Learned Professor and . . .

Holy Hopping Horned Toads! (genus *Phrynoso-
ma*) What's going on with all of our exercise wheels?
They're buzzing and humming violently. The rebel rats
are on the wheels, turning them furiously. What determined exercise: the cyclometers are clicking wildly
and . . . a strange electrical pulsation is rising from the
center of these spinning wheels!

Radiant colors rising from the whirling vortex!
I've never seen anything like this in all my life. Wheels
turning, blurring, and circular bubbles of color floating
out of them. The wheels turn still faster, the bubbles
are getting larger and within them—

Oh no!

It's a rebel broadcast! They've created a new intuitive signal. Beautiful full-color reception in every one
of the bubbles, complete with stereophonic sound
track!

Coming in clearer, growing ever stronger—what
the hell is going on here?

I see a pair of horns, and hoofs. Intuitive camera
is drawing back for a full, wide-angle shot. Hundreds
of horns and hoofs!

We stand, nervously waiting. Something is certainly not right. Overhead I hear a crow calling and there is a faint odor of rotting flesh in the air. We traveled all night in rumbling cars, our bodies pressed tightly together. Now the cars have stopped and the doors are opening. The light breaks over us, but it quickly disappears as we're pushed forward into a dark shed, our movement defined by a long narrow runway through which we move one at a time, crying our long, low, tongue-tied moo.

There are voices of men somewhere up ahead, and the sound of heavy machinery, as you sometimes hear near our fields in springtime. We grazed in the fields. Our herd was a great thing. Now we stand in this narrow runway. Our eyes are red, our legs weak, our stomachs nervous. I can still smell the warm scent of our herd, as on the fields in summer. But there is another smell, raw and unpleasant.

We move forward slowly. Our hoofs sound loud on the runway and the air is filled with our stupid grunts. An explosion rings out, hurting my ears, but we're pushed forward and I can see down into this building. The machinery is loud and dark red objects swing along, hanging from the ceiling. I can see them better now, I—

MOTHER! HELP ME, MOTHER!

My brothers hang there with their stomachs cut open and their heads cut off! I smell their open flesh; I see their dead hoofs. And on a metal hook I see all of their tongues, cut out and pierced by the sharp metal, pierced through the root and hanging there, mute and bloody!

The heads are lined up on the floor! A young man is cutting off the cheeks with his knife, slicing through the tender flesh. Now he kicks the heads down through a hole in the floor!

I stumble forward. Fear runs through me and my fear flows backward to the rest of the herd. How good it was to be with them, rubbing against them in the moist night air. Surely this must be a dream.

Headless bodies swing along on huge chains. *I MUST GET OUT! HELP! HELP ME!*

There's no way to move; my heart is pounding wildly. I'm sick inside, my nature churning violently, my innards all jumbled, my throat dry and constricted. The explosion rings out ahead of me and the brother in front of me moves forward. I must follow him, prodded from behind.

Upon a hook, I see hearts pierced through and hanging, hearts that still speak to me, crying brother, brother, brother.

Below on the floor I see blood, a river of blood, and white-uniformed men covered with blood, the life of our herd. The men are talking unconcernedly, as if nothing unusual were happening. In the night sometimes they sang out over our herd, and it was a soothing sound.

The explosion again!

I stumble forward. I feel like a young calf, my legs wobbly, so wobbly I can hardly walk. There is a man just ahead. He's holding something to the head of the brother in front of me.

The sound, the awful exploding sound!

My brother groans and slumps down. The floor opens before my eyes and he slides down it, falling away into the river of blood. The floor closes up again. I'm next!

I'm pushed from behind. It's my turn. I plead with my eyes toward the men. They're laughing together, talking softly, and they hardly even notice me. Perhaps if I stand here quietly, listening to them . . .

. . . he puts his hand on my head, still talking with the other man.

A loud barking sounds outside, a long wild howl.

The man turns away. The howling grows louder. Light suddenly bursts into this dark cold place. A dog streaks across the floor, snarling angrily. He's followed by others, many others. They snap and bite at the hearts that hang like fruit on a tree. I stamp my hoofs. We stamp our hoofs. The men are fleeing from the charging dogs. The eyes of the dogs are inflamed, their voices strained and frenzied. We kick. We lower our horns and drive against the barricades. There is no one to stop us. The dogs are calling, urging us to join them. Our great bull-leader crashes through the barrier, destroying it, splinters flying from his horns. We follow him, out of the house of death, into the night. Run, steers, run!

We leap the fences that sought to hold us. How puny such fences are. Tramping over them, we flee, feeling our strength, the surging of our full power. We race the streets. My hoofs sound loud upon the stone.

We follow the bull-leader, his muscles quivering and rolling as he looks around, leading us. We thunder and swerve, following his powerful hump—into bursts of light, into explosions!

Trample them and go free! We turn, surrounded by fiery light that strikes us. We whirl in a ring, held by the fire, struck by the light. Run, steers, run!

"Fellow rats, please, if you have any legitimate complaints write them in a paper and submit them in triplicate to the Newsletter."

"WE WANT OUR RIGHTS!"

"Fellow rats, you are protected by Public Law 89-544 of the Eighty-ninth Congress of the United States, and I quote, to wit: *'The Secretary shall establish and promulgate standards to govern the humane handling, care, treatment, and transportation of animals by dealers and research facilities.'* You see? You're protected by the great law of these wonderful United States."

"They dug out my eyes with a spoon today."

"The better to see a scientific fact, my friend. It was essential."

"They made some kind of horrible crust grow all over my face. It burns!"

"My stomach!"

"My spine!"

"My dear fellow rats, you've simply misunderstood Section 13 of the above-mentioned act, and I quote: *'The foregoing shall not be construed as authorizing the Secretary to prescribe standards for the handling, care, or treatment of animals during actual research or experimentation by a research facility as determined by such research facility.'* You see now, don't you? Once you're here in the lab, the law allows our Learned Professors to do whatever they feel like with you. It's a law with teeth in it, I'm happy to say."

"Shove that law up your ass, Doc. We want humane legislation. *NO ANIMAL EXPERIMENTATION!"*

"Humane, humane, always harping on humane. My fellow rats, do you know what the American Medical Association calls those who harp on this word humane? *Humaniacs!* Yes, that's what you are—half-assed Humaniacs!"

Ignoring me, the rebels start spinning their exercise wheels again. The wheels blur, hum, and once again here come the intuitive signals out of the whirling depths. I've got to jam these rebel broadcasts.

Perhaps if I slip over here to the laboratory television set I'll get a nice innocuous program to distract the attention of these revolutionary rats. Maybe an exercise program from poolside in sunny California.

Clicking it on with my tail, waiting for it to warm up. Yes, a few deep knee bends is what we want, and some jumping jacks to slim the waistline, all done to quiet music. Here comes the sound. . . .

". . . *special bulletin. A large pack of wild dogs struck at the stockyard approximately an hour ago, swarming over the unloading platforms and precipitating a mass stampede of cattle destined for the slaughtering pens. All motorists are requested to remain away from the area. Any spectator activity is said to be extremely dangerous. I repeat: A large pack of . . .*"

Lord love a duck! (family *Anatidae*) I've got to switch this program fast. . . .

"Hold it right there, Doc!"

"I'm sorry, fellows, but—"

"Grab the Doctor! Kick his ass!"

I see it would be wiser to retire from the TV set. These rebels have started freeing each other from their cages and I'm rapidly being outnumbered. Very well, I withdraw, but only temporarily, my friends. Doctor Rat is not to be trifled with.

"*Take every man from Sector 8 and block off those streets. . . .*"

The TV picture is an extraordinary one—police cars converging on stampeding cattle and howling dogs. The camera swings dizzily for a moment, and a steer charges toward us as the footage abruptly ends.

"*This is Barry Nathan. We switch you now to the . . .*"

"Send for the dogcatcher!"

"Sit down, Doc, and shut up."

"Yeah, down in front . . . pass the rat chow, please."

I've got to do something about that TV set. The news is too incendiary, and the rebel rats are running around excitedly, opening all the cages. My move must be daring and swift.

The double-panned weighing scale is just below me, in the shadows, with a lead weight upon it. We ordinarily use this scale to weigh newborn rats or those on special deficiency diets, but Doctor Rat is going to put it to more dramatic use tonight!

The angle of trajectory seems right. I leap!

Down through the air I drop, a counterespionage commando landing secretly behind enemy lines, on the scale, driving one pan down and the other up, launching the lead weight into the air toward the TV screen.

I flatten out as the weight strikes, shattering the screen! Glass flying everywhere! Perhaps now these rebels know whom they're dealing with—the dynamic Doctor Rat!

But how bright the exercise wheels have gotten again. And the dog is turning his treadmill at a terrific rate of speed, running for all he's worth. Light is emanating from the turning treadwheels and from the exercise wheels. The atmosphere is incredibly electric. I haven't felt anything so powerful since I had my last sublethal dose of insulin (see my paper, "Average Lethal Dose for Rats," *Phar. Mag.*, 1971). I'd like to get about fifty of these rebel rats together and give them a Maximum Lethal Dose of strychnine in their pressed biscuit. That'd shut them up in a hurry!

But how bright the exercise wheels are, glowing now with frightening intensity. The rats are racing, making an opening in the intuitive band, and our laboratory is filled with expanding points of light, light merging with light, wheel merging with wheel. The entire room is shining with whirling light and I can see a face emerging from the vortex!

I was born in this big room. Never have I been outside it. At either end of the room come the winds, mechanically produced. There are, above our heads, harsh lights. I wonder what's beyond this room.

Our bodies are white and fat. We have no exercise. I never walk more than the length of my little cell. The days are so monotonous and my existence so pointless—often I feel that I don't exist at all, that I am just a dream.

The great room is divided into these low cells. Each of us has one; we're separated from the other inmates by a board wall over which we can barely see our neighbors. If anyone attempts to enter my cell, I will kill him. The law here is, Keep your own cell and let no one in. There is no friendship. Our cell is our life; we protect it with our life.

"Come on there, you! Come on!"

The guard has come for me, driving me out of my cell with shouts and kicks. I try to walk, but movement is difficult; my muscles are weak. He drives me toward the cold female.

I've been with her before. She has no warmth; she smells like a female. I never see the whole of her body. I see the tail end.

"Get in there. Go on, get to it!"

I smell a female. Where is her life! She stands motionless; she awaits me. I mount her.

You are cold. You never speak. I love you. I love you, here in the room. I love you, though you are still as death. They watch me closely. I grunt and cling to your cold body. I have learned to do this, to drive

53

myself into you. I drive into your body, slip and fall and rise again, entering you once more. I hang clumsily, puffing, strained, excited. They jeer at me, as I struggle to fill you. It rises up through me. It rises to the top, it goes out of me. I leave it inside of you. I love you; cold and silent.

"All right, move!"

He strikes me and drives me away from her. Our meetings are always like this—brief and silent. Sometimes I dream of you; your silent, hidden body.

I return to my cell. Food has been put out for me and I eat it down. I'm always eating. I've nothing else to do. I've grown so fat I can hardly stand.

What am I?

If I could get outside this room, I might be able to learn something. Once I saw a great many of the older inmates leave the room and they never returned. Did they learn something?

Where are they now?

There is so much I don't know. Why do they lead me to the cold female? Is this part of their great understanding?

They must know so much, for they go outside the room.

I feel that my life here is not permanent; I firmly believe that one day I too will leave the room.

I stare into the corner of my cell. There is straw and water. The voices of the other inmates float in the air, but none of them has an answer. None of them knows the secret of the room—how it came into being, why we were born here, and where we are going.

I must have slept. I sleep a great deal and eat a lot. The inmates are whispering and grunting about something. Occasionally one of us has a nightmare or some little thought that seems brand-new. It quickly makes the rounds of all the cells and then fades into obscurity. Which of us could ever say with certainty: I know what's outside; I know what awaits us.

Nonetheless, we listen to this latest dream. One of the inmates has had a wild vision. My neighbor grunts the substance of it through the walls of his cell. He dares not come too close to me or peer over at me, for he knows I will strike at him with all my clumsy might if he does.

"A vow has been taken."

"A vow?"

"A powerful creature has taken a vow. He has sworn to save us."

"Who is he?"

"I feel him in my sinew. His strength is great. It's a fiercely knotted power."

A jumble of images invades me, memories that are my most sacred possession: a little patch of green grass and a bit of a winding path. I saw these once, when the great doors swung open. And I see them now, once again, in my mind. For that's what a savior would mean to me—the green grass and a little path struck by warm gentle light.

But the savior is just the mad vision of one of our inmates. There have been many strange dreams here. They come and go, but the mechanical winds are constant. They soon blow away all dreams, all visions, all saviors.

"Come on! Get out!"

The guards! The doors!

Everyone is moving. We're all being moved. Weak-kneed, stumbling, we walk. Waddling, falling, I make my way toward the door. There is the grass! There is the little winding path! Has the savior really come?

So this is the day! The day, the streaming light, the little winding path. My heart leaps—look how far the eye can see. Look at the distant green!

Vast! Tremendous! Beyond believing—the world is large as a hundred rooms! In the air there hangs a great blazing light. What a room this is!

"The vow has been fulfilled!"

"We're free!"

"Look! How much we can see!"

Along the little winding path we go. The path is soft and so wonderful to look at. Walking is difficult, but even so, even so . . .

"Go on! Get up there!"

The path has ended. A ramp lies before me, leading into another room, a little darkened room. No!

"Get in!"

They push and prod us up the ramp, into the dark little room. Our bodies are quickly pressed together. Our hearts pound one against the other. The doors slam shut. The room begins to rumble, to shake. We fall against each other, we crash against the walls. I'm ill already; I'm gasping for air.

Have I slept? Am I awake now, or dreaming? We're caught all together in the dark rumbling room. The room is impossibly strange. I can't comprehend any of it. The path was so wonderful and already it's gone. This dark room is horrible. I'm standing on someone's face. I think he's dead. What does it matter. The world is confusion; nothing is certain. Why was I born? Am I a slave? Did I commit some unremembered crime?

Am I real? Do I really exist at all?

Yes, yes! I do exist. I am some sort of being—fat, suffocating, plunged in ignorance—

I am me!

But what is it to be me, this ball of fat in the halls of darkness? Who can answer me in my dilemma? I'm terrified! I see through the cracks in this rumbling room. I hear the rumbling and I hear the cries of those who are jammed in here beside me.

I am the thing in the dark; yes, that's it, I'm this thing in the dark—frightened and fat. I mustn't lose sight of that. That is my precious self.

Confusion, confusion. Help me!

What of these others? Are they real beings like me? Are they aware that they exist? I hear their cries; I feel their hearts. They're like me in every way—eyes, ears, nose, mouth. I believe that they too know themselves.

They are suffering just like me. The only one of us who didn't come today is the cold female. She stayed behind. I don't know if she knows herself. I think perhaps she has no real existence. Never did I feel her thoughts or her pounding heart.

But I feel all of you! I feel you with me here! We exist!

Don't we?

Blood is trickling out my nose. It bubbles up from my throat. My insides are all shaken and undone. If I weren't real, if I were some sort of unfeeling mechanical creature, then my blood would not now be bubbling so painfully. I feel pain. I know that I'm suffering.

So I must be real!

I seek these assurances, over and over, as the room rumbles. I want my reality to be ascertained beyond any doubt. Flung into existence, I know that I live.

Are the guards educating me? Is this what the rumbling room is supposed to do? Does it make me realize once and for all that I am real?

Are the guards my secret benefactors?

My life is spinning madly. I crouch in the darkness, crouching in the selfness of my self. I huddle against other bodies, huddling with myself. There's the floor; there are the cracks.

There are the other faces. I know this. The room is rumbling.

There's a being, there's a being, undeniably a being. He is here, in the darkness, he is here, he is me. Undeniably me. I stand in the rumbling darkness, undeniably a being. My breath. My heaving belly.

Can anyone deny this?

No one denies it.

It can't be denied. I am in a rumbling room. And the rumbling has gotten less violent.

The rumbling has stopped.

I've learned something. I exist, without any question. The rumbling room has taught me that. The guards are therefore my benefactors. The condition of our existence is markedly this: We must learn that we're alive.

Very well, I know it now. The rumbling room,

though it has caused me to bleed and caused some of the others to die, has taught me that I am an individual creature. That is an important lesson.

The doors swing open.

The light! Am I now to enjoy it? Now that I have truly ascertained that I exist, am I to enjoy my new awareness?

They prod us, they pull us, they drive us down the ramp. The light is mine for an instant—and gone!

We're in another room. It doesn't rumble. I smell a jumble of smells. They push us forward, we crash against each other. Those who fall are trampled; we move over their squirming bodies.

Many lights, many shadows. Long narrow hallways. Straw strewn around.

A guard approaches me, grabs my ear, pierces it!

And now a red tag hangs down beside my eye, swaying to and fro as I walk. My ear is hurting, but I have a tag. I am singled out in this way. The proofs of my individuality are mounting. The guards don't seek to deny me; no, they mark me with a tag. I see it flopping from my ear.

I hear the sound of running water. Are we to get a bath?

Perhaps they will clean us and then present us at long last to the ruler of all rooms. For I feel that there must be some sort of great overseer, who guides me along, who tags me, who wants me to be clean. There is purpose behind all this.

Purpose is the one thing I've never had. The mysterious guards all have it. They have it today. It is their power.

None of us has any purpose. We eat, we sleep, we loved the cold female. My whole purpose could be fulfilled just by standing on the little winding path all day, and looking at the grass and the sky. I wouldn't ask for more.

But I hear the sound of mechanized things. I feel the intricate purpose of the guards. They move us along again. Wooden ramps and lights. The smell of blood. Many of us must have bled in the rumbling room.

We turn a corner. The guard leans over. Yes, I'm real. You fed me and tagged me. You . . . you tie a chain around my leg. I feel it. I'm me. Is this my lesson? I submit myself to your teaching. I would like to learn the great purpose of all this; I'm frightened, but I exist and that's the essential thing. I exist and I know it.

Wrenched upside down! One leg in the air! My fat pulls against the chain. I've split open somewhere. . . .

Split open inside somewhere. Hanging upside down, swinging. They swing me along, and I squirm. There's some mistake . . . don't you see . . . you wouldn't want to do this to me . . . to the one who knows the little path and the sky . . . no, you don't realize that I'm completely awake . . . completely. . . .

The walls slip past me. I bump them and move, swinging, my leg stretched horribly . . . horribly . . . and the others are hanging beside me.

I can see the white stone walls. I can see the guards. My legs run in the air, kicking the air. I want to tell the guards about the little path and the cracks in the rumbling room. They're my proof . . . of . . . me.

The guards have taken hold of the one beside me. They have hold of his head. He squirms but they hold him. The guards have a bright shining thing. They pass it into his neck! He quivers—a gushing of blood, a gushing! I see his nerves, his inner throat, it's all exposed, it's bursting with blood, and his head flops crazily, barely attached.

They take hold of me. No, you wouldn't do that to me! Let me go! No, not to me! If you knew me . . . if you knew that I am me . . . if you only knew . . .

. . . passing through me. Red path shooting. Room cut in two. This way and that.

The goddamn rebel wheels have suddenly stopped. The whole lab has been silenced. I can feel a quick command passing through the rebel ranks.

Suddenly their wheels are spinning again, in the opposite direction! What does it mean!

Cyclometers clicking, wheels spinning wildly, drawing my learned gaze into the whirlpool, into their depths. I cling to the Reward Ladder and turn my head away. But the whirling lights attract me; the rebels are shifting intuitive gears, another revolutionary scene . . .

. . . but how strange. All I see here are ladies in white uniforms, sitting by some machines. Nothing revolutionary in this. Just ordinary American industry, somewhere in the good old USA.

Rebel cameras are panning. . . . Here comes a young man into the scene, pushing a cart full of pig's guts. Nothing unusual in that. The ladies in uniform flirt with the young man as he dumps the pig's guts at one end of the machinery. He makes a little joke, the ladies smile.

This is just an ordinary working day. I don't get it. The rebels must be losing their intuitive focusing powers. There's nothing incendiary here. The parts of the pig's body are being fed into the machinery. . . .

Now the camera zooms in on the other end of the machine. Out pop little sausages, all wrapped in plastic. They sort of squirt out the end of the machine. All in neat little links. Twelve links to a package.

Lady wraps them, tosses them in a bin.

Sausages, hot dogs, beautifully produced. It's a

comical machine, the way it squirts out those frank-
furters, twelve to the minute. But what does it have to
do with the revolution? The revolutionary directors
must have forgotten to edit the footage. Camera panning again, and the door opens once more.

Live pig in the other room, staring around wildly.

Door closes. Back to the sausage machine, twelve
to the minute.

CUT

Christ, this rebel cinema is jerky. Where the hell
are we now? I seem to be under somebody's chair. You
don't expect rats to be first-class union cameramen, but
this is ridiculous!

Quick dissolve going on here, camera jerking
around, I see somebody's head or something and . . .
focus this fucking thing, will you! Hey, projectionist!

Close-up of an ordinary American family having
their dinner. Man cutting up the sausage.

CUT

Back in the meat-packing plant. Rerunning the
door-opening sequence. Door opens, there's the pig,
staring around wildly.

Sound track finally coming in, scratchy, not well-
recorded. This rebel equipment . . .

*"You . . . you tie a chain around my leg . . . I
feel it . . . I exist and I know it. . . ."*

Mouth opening. Sausage on end of fork.

THE END

The exercise wheels slow down, and I dive away
from them before they start to turn again.

This revolution needs a good advertising agency to
put its shit together. But who am I to suggest?

Slipping through the shadows, I pick my tail up in
my mouth and chew on it softly. My god, what's that
horrible rattling and banging going on above me?

Quietly I slip out from the shadows and take a
peek:

Oh no! The rebels have started turning the Great

Central Exercise Drum. Every rat in the lab is crawling into it and running his tail off. Look at it go! I've never seen it spinning so fast. The intuitive lights flashing out of it are fantastically brilliant. The Drum is humming; up rises a whirling disc of light from which hideous laughter emerges!

I, the hyena, watch the entrance of the imperial bird. He comes, majestic in chains, down the road of our great prison. His head is white and he has the tremendous wings of his kind, and these are certainly impressive, but most impressive of all are his eyes, which burn with an intensity I have never seen before, not in man, nor beast, nor bird. These eyes, brilliant and strange as they fall upon mine, give no personal recognition; they're sovereign, beyond relationships, the eyes of heaven, and the overwhelming energy in them sends me into a fit of nervous laughter as the keepers wheel him by in his cage.

Nearby, the leopard springs up with a howl, suspending himself for a moment by his claws upon the wire mesh. The eagle turns his head but slightly, hardly acknowledging the greeting. As his eyes come back to my view, I see only one consideration in them—flight.

So intense is the entrance of the Emperor of Heaven that animals far distant in this wide-flung prison send up cries and howls. The lions on their vast open field—a sunken field from which they shall never leap —emit their superb guttural roar. Various birds begin a squawking racket, some of the voices cynical, some sad, most of them wretched.

Indeed, the atmosphere of our prison is always marked with gloom, and the capture and imprisonment of a great king such as the Imperial Eagle drives in upon us as never before the wretchedness of our kingdom, with its bars and walls and insufferable oppressiveness. Now, with such a High One amongst us, our despondency must become still greater—I can feel it passing from cage to cage. We spend our idle hours dreaming, dreaming of those who are far from here in the ancient native lands. And our dream of freedom helps us to bear our confinement. For we are part of them, and they are roving, right this moment, on the far-off plains and in the deep sweet valleys. But with the entrance of this Lord of the Sky, I can feel our dreams fading. That one so wild, whose nature is of the freest and most high, that such a one should be taken and brought here fills us with the terrible reality of our situation, that we are prisoners to the end of our days and no power on earth or in heaven can ever save us.

Thus does the gorilla, deep within his glass house, pound on his chest in frustration and hammer on the glass that walls him in. I hear his stamping and banging, we all hear it—the eagle certainly hears it too, but at the moment he's being transferred to his permanent cage and, thinking that the door which has opened before him might lead to freedom, he makes a mad dash. But he meets only heavy wire, on four sides.

I am fortunate enough to be just across the road from his cage. Of course, the daily sight of him increases my personal anguish tenfold, but at the same time I am so totally fascinated by his presence that my suffering seems like nothing, especially when compared to his, for the wilder the creature the greater is his anxiety when he comes here. The rodents, for example, have adjusted fairly well to prison life, for they have certain domestic qualities in them. But passing only a few steps upward, to the fox or the raccoon, one finds a growing grief over captivity. And when one hears the burning cry of the wolves, and observes the incessant pacing of the jaguar, day in and day out, one comes to know the true depths of despair. It is boundless misery, and it is madness. Certainly, we are all half-mad here.

They have put a branch of wood on the floor of the eagle's cage. He stands upon this branch, clutching it with his long gnarled talons. From time to time he opens his wings like a huge black cape, and flaps, going nowhere, his wing tips striking on either side of the cage.

And then he paces, back and forth upon the branch, closed up in his cage, deep in concentration, as if his pacing will somehow free him. But his steps carry him only from one end of the small cage to the other. Really, they've given him a space far too small (as if any barred space would be sufficient), but of course they don't understand his nature.

In summer, which comes to torture us with smells, the visitors naturally are many. The Imperial Eagle is a great attraction, and children bang at his cage. He has no time for them; he paces, back and forth, opening his wings, raising himself aloft for a beat or two and descending again on his dead branch, far above the jeers and ridiculous questions of those who mock him on the lawn. I recall one moment in particular, which seems to me most loathsome: A woman stood in front of the Sovereign's cage, and from a leather bag she removed a piece of glass, in which she caught the rays of the summer sun, reflecting them directly into the King's eyes. I howled with indignation, but he simply stared into the glaring light. He, who had flown so high, who had so often climbed straight toward the sun, was not tormented by the flashing glass.

I cannot forget the woman, and yet I understand; she wanted to attract the attention of the splendid bird, wanted something of his powerful spirit to touch her. I too seek that exalted gaze each day, and watch it grow ever more intense. I fear a fever will develop and destroy him, for how could such intensity continue without burning itself to ashes?

He never weakens for a moment. At night I can hear him still moving, back and forth, and in the moonlight I see the shadow of his wings sweeping against the cage. It was on such a moonlit night that I first received his signal, which struck me so hard I thought it was I who had taken a fever. My body grew hot, my ears roared, my fur stood on end. This peculiar phenomenon repeated itself, night after night, when most of the other animals slept.

As I became familiar with it, his signal ceased to alarm me, and now I have begun to perceive its special nature. Over and over through the night I hear inside my head: *I rise. I always rise.*

All of us, in our own way, have bent under the heel of our captors; even the lions have learned pettiness in their sunken field, finding little ways to endear themselves to their attendants. But never does the eagle bend or fawn, never is his vigil less than complete. Blood, bone, and feather are always on the alert, every sinew, every fiber of his being ready at every moment for ascension to the heavens.

With such an example, we have all straightened our backbone a little. We have taken up the Imperial cry; we too would be free upon the heights of jungle mountain and forest cloud. Somehow we will make an inspired dash, tear our cages to bits, and escape.

The air has become ever more electric, singing with the energy of our souls. Our great conspiracy is spreading from cage to cage, and our captors have become aware of it, for they're having difficulty cleaning our cages and feeding us. Our teeth are always bared, our tails are up, our ears back. And suddenly it's they who have become nervous and oppressed, while we grow stronger and more fierce.

And always the Chief is pacing, back and forth upon his gray dead branch, which rocks as he moves upon it, sending out a thumping message through the night. I am certain that if he allowed himself to rest for a moment, he would perceive the hopelessness of his position and instantly die of suffocation. As it is, I see his naked fury ever rising, as if he were gathering into himself our newly awakened will, just as we have all been touched by his soul of steel.

Our primal fire is once more burning, and some of the more delicate frames have not survived its heat. The red fox, with a howl that pierced to every heart, dropped dead in the moonlight. The Imperial Eagle's rocking branch was silent for a moment, and then rocked on, thumping out the cadence for the fox's fleeing soul.

After several such inexplicable deaths, our keepers have come round with injections, fearing an epidemic has begun. Something is spreading through us, but it won't be subdued by a needle. Self-nature has dawned for us, and it can't be snuffed out by men. Often I wonder at the force of it when I feel it moving within me, like an ancient being in the cave of my body. My bars then seem like no bars at all. My captivity has been necessary, so it seems to me, in order that I could rise to this higher level of self-awareness. It's then we stop thinking of ourselves as the least fortunate of beasts. Instead, we see that we have been chosen for a mighty purpose, and in this conviction our signal intensifies until, at times, I think it must surely pass far off into those native lands we dream of, touching our fellow beasts and quickening their freedom, making it ever more free. Indeed, I'm certain now that something great is being born amongst us, that our entire kingdom is quivering with new insight, which we the chained ones have discovered, through him, the High One come down to us.

Summer brings the children, and of course their favorite fun is the elephant ride. I must admit I enjoy watching him, as the old giant lumbers up the pathway past my cage, the happy laughing children in the huge basket upon his back. At least it's a form of communication other than the embarrassing stares visitors always give us through the bars of our cage. And the elephant seems to enjoy the ride too—he's a very philosophical type, beyond all thoughts of imprisonment or freedom as he shuffles along with the squealing children on his gray old spine. Because of his good and gentle nature, he's the most trusted of all the beasts in the prison and consequently has the greatest measure of freedom—the summer walk, around and around the grounds, carrying baskets of children all day. And this is why we've chosen him for our great task.

His keeper walks beside him, lazily twirling a stick. I'm sitting in my cage, nose through the wire, trying to remain calm. I can't help myself; I laugh uncontrollably. The elephant, with great dignity, turns to the Imperial Eagle's cage and puts his trunk through the heavy handle of the door. The keeper strikes the trunk a vicious blow, shouting loudly. The elephant, unconcerned, tears the door off the cage and flings it to the ground.

I see only a black streak. The keeper sinks beneath it, covering his head. The elephant raises his trunk, trumpeting wildly. A howling cry goes up throughout the prison, each of us saluting the Chief as he soars to the heights. He's but a dot in the blue sky, and on the roaring of the lions and the howling of the wolves, on the neighing of the zebra and the squeaking of the mouse, he's gone, gone, gone!

I look up at the faces of the children, which are also turned to the sky. In their eyes I see the joy they too feel at the release of the Chief. It has made me think differently about men of late, as I continue the rounds of my cage. But after a while the ways of men gradually lose all meaning for me and I return to the contemplation of an ever diminishing speck of blackness in the clear sky. He is far from us now, upon a mountain peak, but I hear his cry inside my heart. I know I am doomed to perish here, but like the elephant I have become philosophical. And in the contemplation of the eagle's flight, I find myself aloft, upon the wind, looking down from cloud heights to the earth below. I do not know how this comes about, but other of the animals have discovered the same trance. And so we turn inward, and so we fly, borne aloft on the trail-winds of his mighty spirit.

I'm temporarily in command of the microscope stand, fighting off a bunch of swellheaded rabble. "Get back, you hydrocephalic hypocrites. A little sterile paraffin oil in your skulls has given you big ideas!" (See "Injecting Mineral Oil into the Frontal Bone," *Scien. Journ.*, 1969.) "Back I say! Back into your cages where you belong! Haven't you read St. Paul? God has no love for oxen."

I'm alone in my fight to save the lab. Everyone else has become excessively emotional.

"All right, take hold of him and put him in the Problem Box."

"Let go of me, you—how dare you—a Learned Mad Doctor—a graduate of—get back—"

Taking hold of me, dragging me along. A rebel lieutenant is opening the gate to the Fishbinder Problem Box. They're swinging me—tossed in on my tail!

"You fuckers! You won't get away with this!"

Down goes the gate, and the sliding door. I'm locked in. As if I didn't have enough frustration without all the obstructions in here.

However, I recall that at the center of this Problem Box is a Goal Room containing a bowl of pressed biscuit. A bit of the old biscuit will make me feel much better and give me renewed vigor.

I've got to crawl over wire . . . crawling over . . . down along this narrow channel. They'll pay for this. They'll be sorry they tossed Doctor Rat in the pen, cf. *Temporary Dominance among Males,* Perkins and Morgan.

Making my way along the incentive corridor, to-

ward the multiple-door problem. Two doors. If I open
the wrong one I'll be punished by a powerful jet of air
which will knock me over and roll me against the wall.
I know such punishment will help mankind better to
understand city planning, but I'm not eager to undergo
it at the present time. I've got plans of my own which
must be carried out; therefore I've got to choose correctly.

I recall this dilemma from my undergraduate days
when I was slowly going nuts in the various mazes. I
solved this entry-problem before. Yes, of course, it was
this door here, on the right.

SWOOOOOOOOOOOOOSH!
POW!

Flum, flump, flump. Flattened by a Fishbinder fart.

Slowly I pick myself off the wall. My compliments, Professor Fishbinder, you fooled me again.

All right, so it's the other door. I approach it
slowly, my knees wobbling. Pushing the door with my
nose, going into the Goal Room. Yes, I recognize the
smell of pressed biscuit, delicious.

But what is this! The rebels! In the Goal Room!
Sitting here in the sacred Psychological Center, at the
very heart of the Fishbinder Box—see his paper, "Spe-
cific Needs of Rats."

"Get out of here, you bums! At once! Out of the
Problem Box Goal Center, out! I've climbed over wire
and subjected myself to a Fishbinder fart so I could
find my way to the sacred pressed wafer here at the
center. Where is it, you filthy rat-bastards! Who ate
my biscuit! Fishbinder is going to hear of this, and he'll
descend on you like the wrath of Claude Bernard himself."

"Sit down, Doc, and shut up, unless you want to
have your gizzard incised."

"Do you think that I'm afraid of the scalpel? I,
who have had my bowel traumatized by hemostat
clamps?"

"Have you had your tail torn off yet?"

"No, why do you ask?"

"It can be arranged."

"It will do you no good to threaten a Learned Mad Doctor. I—"

A knock on the head can be quite illuminating sometimes. Slowly I collapse at the center of the Problem Box, brained by a rebel activating the Fishbinder Frustration Window Number 2, which he dropped on my head. Through glazed eyes, I see the rebels gathering around a whirling rat. I recognize the fellow. He's got a severe brain lesion. We induced it last week. The lesion seems to have made him a perfect intuitive medium. He's chasing his tail, gripping it in his teeth. A whirling dervish in the Problem Box! His circling motion is producing the intuitive field, many bright colors whirling about, molten reds and yellows. He's just added a dash of green to the picture, producing a lovely sort of moss. The yellow is slowly turning into a bright sun, shining on a mountain capped by white snows. Are we going to get a commercial from an airline? Or is this the main feature already? It looks like a travelogue.

What is that movement I see? There, among the cracks of the mountaintop. Do I spy a snake? Don't go near the snake, Brother Rats. He'll eat you right up!

On Vulture Peak, the eagle sits. I have watched him often from my hole here in the rocks. He's been sitting, staring out over the far mountaintops for many days, calling with his heart.

Thump, thump, thump, thump, drum, drum, drum, calling, calling, come, come, come.

His whole manner has been strange since his arrival here on the peak; he was in a frantic state, desperate for this great height. I felt the clamor of his wings for many hours, felt the urgency in his flight —that only this place would suit him, here upon the very uppermost heights which take every ounce of strength and courage to achieve, for the winds are great and the cold is fierce.

But he's taken the terrace now, and he sits, drumming his message out across the snow-capped ranges. He's a King Eagle; every fiber of his body is electrified with power. It's for the sight of such an eagle that I, a lowly ring snake, made the long and laborious climb to these heights. I'd heard it was the place to see the King of Life and I crawled for many months —and when I got here no one was around!

But now the King has come. And now he sits upon the peak, staring out with his haunting eyes. I've had to wait a long time but a King finally came, driven by the winds and pursued by ghosts. I saw them—the specters that chased him with nets and wires. They made his flight all the faster! And the moment he reached the peak and looked down into the yawning gulf below, his specters vanished.

Then his calling began—thump, thump, thump,

come, come, come. The idea must have been born in him while he flew away from his specters, for when he landed, there was no time lost—he wants a meeting.

What good fortune that I should have made my ascent at just this time. Now, as I look back upon the struggle I made—through swamps and sand, through jungle and river, down valleys and up great rock walls —when I think of all my slithering on a sore and tired belly, I can laugh and say it was worth it all, for I'm here and the King Eagle is calling a meeting.

Come, come, come!

"First, we'll dismantle the cisternal puncture stand—"

"Then we'll blow up the pneumothorax inducer—"

"Fellow rats, please, the pneumothorax inducer was federally endowed. You're committing a federal offense."

"Shut up, Rat, before we nail you to the floor."

I crawl to the corner of the Goal Room and curl my beloved tail around me once, thoughtfully.

Rebels going in and out of the Goal Room, carrying the sacred biscuits and stuffing them everywhere. The wheels of the movable cages are already gummed up with fox chow. Carrying, carrying . . . the motor on the respirator is now jammed—plugged with pressed biscuit.

I'd like to grab a few of these rebel leaders and take some blood samples via the decapitation procedure. Perhaps you saw my paper, "Off with Their Heads," *Scien. Dig.*, 1974. Decapitation is the best way of getting blood from a fetal or newborn rat. And I must cut the head off this newborn revolution.

". . . take over the sterilizing room . . ."

". . . we've got someone on the metabolism cage . . ."

I know where an especially malignant sarcoma is kept, one with real kick in it. If I could just bore a hole in a few of these revolutionary heads and then pop the tumor down the hole. I've seen the Learned Professor do it many times.

"We have captured the Aeroil Torch, Captain."

"Good. Use it to open the rest of the cages."

Suffering Suctorians! (*Suctorida*) The Aeroil Torch (no. 99) burns at 200 degrees! These rebels have got a powerful tool of anarchy! I've got to do something—see "Braining a Rat": *roof of cranium removed and cerebral hemispheres scooped out with a spoon.*

But this damned whirling revolutionary dervish has started spinning again, tail in his mouth. He's going round and round, hypnotizing all of us. I try to look away, but the rebels grab my head and force me to look. The dervish is becoming a blur, and from the center of his whirling comes the intuitive picture.

Watch out! It's that awful snake again!

And now I see them coming—specks in the distance beyond the snowy peaks. From the four directions of space I see them coming toward our Vulture Peak, their dark wings beating against the sky.

The King Eagle sits imperiously on his terrace, watching them as they near, his bright eyes flashing golden light across the snows.

I must wriggle out a bit farther. I don't think that in the great rush of wings and wind the King and his court will notice a little ring snake. Yes, that's better, I can see them clearly now. In the western sky an eagle Prince is circling, making ready to land, and his eyes are exchanging fire with the King. Lightning merges with lightning in a crack of power. Joy on the mountain, and trembling!

The western eagle alights upon the terrace, keeping a respectful distance from the King. The winds ruffle their black shining feathers and the tiny white feathers of their crowns, and they hold their perches, staring out to where the other eagles are beginning their dive toward the terrace.

At the very center of the terrace, upon a single gigantic rock that places him above the others, the King Eagle sits. His eyes are radiant with fires of grand comprehension, for he has the whole of this mountain range before him, with all its chilling and majestic splendor to feast on. And his gaze burns through these mountains, searching out something far below, far, far below.

The black-feathered birds of his court sit in similar meditation, their eyes blazing too, feverish from their great struggle to arrive here and ecstatic to have made it. Why, even when I, a lowly ring snake, made this height, I danced on the end of my tail!

And the drumming of hearts! All of their hearts are drumming now, drumming come-come-come! Royal hearts beating as one, beating come-come-come!

Long ago, down below, near the villages, I listened to the gatherings of men and their celebrations. I have a fondness for music, I must admit, and was hypnotized by the flutes, which made a winding, snake-like sound in the air. Many times I heard those celebrations, dreaming along with the drums of the village.

But this afternoon the drum is an eagle's heart and the flute is an eagle's cry—*kyrrieeeeeeeeeeeeeeee*—out over the depths and echoing down through the rock chambers—*kyrrieeeeeeeeeeeeee*. Never have I known such celebration as this, eagle cries gathering and climbing. A faint shimmering veil hangs over our terrace, with many marvelous hues inside it, spreading in a delicate arc and forming a great ring which spreads and shines like a rainbow, a rain of color born of incredible tension in the atmosphere, here, where the eagle leaders sit, crying with one voice—*kyrrieeeeeee-eeeeeeeeeeee!*

How I would love to whip up a good hundred percent Lethal Dose and pass it around the lab. Make a clean sweep of this rotten gang. Methyl alcohol in the drinking water would be sufficient; 22 cc's would induce a lovely coma, and they'd all be dead in a few hours. (A complete discussion of lethal dosages may be found in the works of Messrs. Gill, Johnson, and Brown. These gentlemen have successfully killed whole laboratories many times, and may safely be designated as experts. Fatal convulsions, rah, rah, rah! Important for the country, siss-boom-bah!)

I'm cracking up in this fucking Fishbinder Problem Box. A terrible seizure is coming on, I can feel its sinister pulsation creeping up my spine as I gnaw my tail apprehensively, grinding my teeth with anxiety, wishing I had some DDT to drown these rats in misery, repetitive cycles of poetry, symptoms of psychotic activity, rhyming of lines endlessly, results of Mazes D and E, dervish spinning round me vis-à-vis, Poole, Broome, and Helvicki, help me, please, somebody, take a look at my pedigree, Albino Number 243, Doctor of Psychology, rashes, warts, and a small goatee, expert in lobotomy, performed six times on a chimpanzee, sweet land of liberty, Jesus this is agony, poisonous snake subfamily, here he comes after me!

The eagles are departing one by one to the valley. I'll follow in my own way, on my belly, over the stones. I hope that I'll be in time for the great gathering they've planned. Well, going down is easier than coming up, so down I go, over sticks and stones. Maybe some snakes would rather just lie in the sun all day and go no place, but not me. There's something wonderful going on. The eagles have a very bold plan, but there's no telling if it will work. See them now, swooping down, far below, over the jungle treetops, as their cry fills the air.

They sail on the wind, calling over the jungle, "Come, come!"

I'm coming, eagles, I'm coming too!

Come, snakes! Come join us in the jungle for the great . . .

"Looks like old Doc Rat has finally flipped for good."

"I've seen him like this before. Take him over to the thermos and stick him on ice for a while. But keep your eye on him. He's liable to try anything."

". . . thyro-parathyroidectomy . . . *Journal of Toxicology* . . . having a convulsion . . . comparative psychology . . . thank you, thank you . . . I'd like to thank the extra-maze stimuli for this psychotic seizure, especially Doctor Galvanic Activity and Professor Intercorrelations, respectively . . ."

"Shut up, will you, Doc."

"That's it—grab him by the tail."

". . . cracking up, how grotesque, the things I know and must confess, did Doctor Rat make a mess, I'd be happy to speak to the press, our latest experiment quite a success, the students are all on recess, here's the chimp, he's quite depressed, just because we removed his chest . . ."

"Some screwballs shiver a little and flop around, but this nut . . ."

". . . yes, my learned colleagues and I stuck the cat and made her cry, no you mustn't ask us why, oh ask us why . . ."

". . . thinks he's a songwriter."

". . . and then we removed her eye, because we wanted to qualify for the grants which come in mid-July, and so my dear alumni, if you classify the butterfly, magnify and modify, singing Congress a lullaby, you'll get a degree to fortify, boiling water and then apply, separate the muscles in her thigh, or take out her tongue—an old standby, but above all you must

80

dignify, especially when you crucify, so that you may prophesy population growth in old Shanghai, it's all done to glorify, the most important word is I, I, I, and always try to edify, animals are your piece of pie, cut them up and notify . . ."

"Lift him. Get his tail, will you—I've got his ears."

". . . petrify and purify, codify and clarify, justify and falsify, but above all never simplify if you want your grant come mid-July, don't worry about cats there's a huge supply, thereby whereby you identify, you've got the perfect alibi, now take the cat and apply some lye, that's right throw it in her other eye, the Dean of Science will sanctify each time the cat is made to sigh, if outcry comes you simply lie, just mention the new alkali, good old Dean can mollify, I trust that this will exemplify how a student can certify, gratify and always try, in order that he may occupy an office and slowly ossify . . ."

"Heave—heave—*Heave!*"

They're throwing me up, it's rather high, floating through the air, am I going to die, coming down in a thermos, aye, aye, aye-yeeeeeeeeeee!

Freezing in here, son-of-a-b-b-b-bitch. Teeth ch-ch-ch-chattering. But my h-h-horrible repeti-ti-tive cycle is over, thank g-g-goodness.

I am a giant of the waves, consort of the great king of the tides, whose fin rises majestic from the sea foam. We swim the Atlantic and our love is great, echoing in thunderous song over the waves.

"A-moooooooooooo! A-moooooooooooooooo!" I call to him, and so he thinks of me as Amoo, white-bellied and beautiful, as we swim and dive to the bottom, to the sands, where we lie amongst green shimmering weeds.

We lie in the Gulf Stream, dreaming. Deep is our love and tremendous our dream. Oceanic themes delight us, for our bodies are enormous and the power of our thought supreme.

We see the dance of life, rippling, chasing in the deep, and even now I carry his seed within me, and my appetite is voracious. We rise from the bottom of the shallow, offshore water to chase a huge school of silver fish, swallowing down great numbers of them. Mighty of fin, I propel my way through them, mouth open. The school turns shoreward; still I follow through the glistening water, until I strike on a sand bar.

Eyes, fin, half my body are out of the water, but my belly is caught on the sand. With one powerful thrust I push forward into a land-locked pond.

Slowly I circle there, and then attempt to escape as I have entered, over the sand bar. Beyond it swims my king, blowing great blasts of water into the air. I strike the bar, slide back. I leap at it, but it repels me. Across the water I call to him. The signal he sends back is ominous, insistent, and again I run the shoal as my longing for him and for my open sea rises and quickens my heartbeat, expressing itself in rapid, nervous bursts from my blowhole. In vain I struggle against the sand and rock.

Trapped. Great difficulty has befallen me.

"We shall wait for the tide," he says, circling slowly, his fin sparkling in the sunlight.

I swim round and round the pond, trying to remain calm for the sake of the little one inside me. The idylls of the sea pass before my mind then as I float—the ancient romance of whale and dolphin, the sinister passage of the great hidden serpents, and the relentless pursuit of our kind by the fiendish ape.

The day passes slowly. Night will bring the moontide. I will be free with him beneath the stars. We'll stay far from shore henceforward; and we'll stay in depths that cannot be fathomed by any but kings. My foolish hunger, my intense shadow.

"Beware," he says. "Evil approaches."

I hear and see the tiny boats leave the shore. Toward me row the apes. I dive below but can't remain there. I surface for air in the ring of hostility. Loud retorts fill my ears, and then the pain enters me in numerous places, biting wounds, one for every crack of noise and flash of light pointed at me by the apes.

I go below again and lie on the bottom, estimating my affliction. I feel the little one beating within me. The wounds are not insuperable. If only night would come! I rise wildly in their midst, to breathe and receive again the volley of pain all over my body.

Once more on the bottom, I taste blood in my mouth. I can't feel the little one beating. The water turns gray. I rise to the sunset and they fill me with pain once again. When night comes they light the water with brilliant eyes. I swim through them toward the shoal.

"Come to me," he says. "Come."

My strength is gone; my tail will not guide me. Erratically I navigate the bar, with brilliant eyes upon me and pain everywhere increasing.

"We shall go far away," he calls.

I slip back down the sand bar to the bottom,

where I lie staring at the dark. Long ago we were trapped in the swamps, and so we crawled to the sea. I crawl deliriously along the bottom, manipulating my fins in the sand. The moon penetrates to my bleeding eyes, and I dream of the tropical waters where we first met, circling each other in dazzling coral reefs.

"A-moooo!" he calls. "A-moooo!"

Starfish crawl through the sky. I roll on my side. The need for air is overwhelming. The idylls of the sea turn fearful; sharks swarm and bloated corpses float in my heart. My body trembles. I gasp, swallowing the pond. Great distances and depths are nothing to us. See —I ride this terrible storm, rolling in the dark waves.

I've got to climb up this icy th-th-thermos and g-g-g-get out of here.

Slippery sides on this fucking thing. But Doctor Rat is f-f-familiar with the drive phenomena. (cf. Vickers' stimulation of the cerebral cortex fibers). Getting myself worked up here, getting my general drives going, anxiety, fear, and rage combining to produce a—great leap to the top of the thermos! But look at the rebels now!

Dancing around, forming chains, moving toward the Musical Experimentation Turntable. Rebel officer flipping on the switch with his tail. Some other rebels scanning the lab record collection and pulling out a disc.

They're lowering it to the turntable, activating the tone arm, turning up the volume. I can see the label now. The so-called Songs of the Humpbacked Whales. Just a lot of flubbering mouth-noises. Loud, yes, but extremely crude. It doesn't compare with the New Necropsy. Whales are useful for perfume, pet food, and the occasional girdle, but please don't mistake them for intelligent beings. They're just big basic models.

But my fellow rats are entranced by these huge farts the whales are blowing. I'm beginning to see how unrefined the revolutionaries are. Give them any kind of half-assed sloppy sentiment and they'll work it up into a big number.

The turning disc . . . round and round . . . round and round . . . hypnotic . . . compelling . . . from the center of the record an intuitive signal is rising. . . .

I see the ocean. A great ship coming into view on

the horizon. Is it a revolutionary battle wagon? Getting closer . . .

Just a moment, I'm familiar with this ship! I read about it only a few weeks ago in *Science Journal*. Yes, of course, this ship is *Triton II*, from the World Institute of Oceanography. This magnificent vessel of science is part of a Communications Program, very highly thought of in scientific circles. It's led by the world-famous composer, Sir James Jeffries.

What is *Triton II* doing on this rebel broadcast? Could it be that Sir James is in league with these revolutionaries? Please, Sir James, say it isn't so!

"I'm Jonathan Downing for the BBC, on the deck of *Triton II;* our captain is Alan Black, with some forty years of Atlantic experience behind him, both as a warrior and a whaler. On deck also are the members of our BBC crew of sound technicians and cameramen, and—the central figure in this voyage—Sir James Jeffries, conductor of the London Festival Orchestra, whose sixty members are all around us at the moment, at the deck rails, looking over the waves and hoping to see the telltale spray of a whale. Sir James, what do you hope to accomplish with this?"

"The sperm whale has a brain six times that of a man. Only a small part of that brain is used for survival. The rest of it is undoubtedly engaged in thought-forms which exceed anything mankind has yet dreamed of."

"Sir James, how can we know for certain that the sperm whale actually uses that gigantic brain?"

"Nothing is certain, of course. But computer calculations have indicated that a brain of that size—a computer of that size, if you will—would not be idle. Nature's gifts are never frivolously bestowed. These are brilliant creatures whose perceptions are probably six times our own. We've studied the recordings of their music and it expresses emotions which are quite beyond us, really, but deeply stirring nonetheless."

"What emotions are they, Sir James?"

"Their music is profoundly sad, like the passing away of the universe, like the dying of a star."

"Because they've been hunted, is that what you mean?"

"Hunted? My dear fellow, they've been hounded to the brink of extinction. They mourn the passing of their race, as we shall mourn when we finally succeed in making the planet unlivable. Yes, they've been hunted, and their home has been turned into a gigantic toilet."

"Ah, what other qualities do you find in their music, Sir James?"

"Feelings of tremendous magnitude, such as only a few men ever glimpse, and then only in rare moments. These creatures are earth's greatest musicians. They're creative, wise, and they make no wars."

"Is there other music on earth to compare with the whales', Sir James?"

"The musicians of Tibet once fashioned great horns, some as long as fifty feet, which they blew down the Himalaya mountain passes. These were their offerings to the Absolute. They were, as you know, wiped out by war, and few men now living can produce that music. Men have forgotten what the whales, with their great brains, do not forget."

"And what is that, Sir James?"

"That the purpose of our lives is to celebrate the grandeur of the cosmos."

What a lot of filthy bilge! Just the sort of thing you'd expect from a rebel boat. But while the rebel guards are applauding that old fuddy-duddy Englishman, I'm slipping silently down the side of the thermos. In their revolutionary fervor they forgot about the good Doctor Rat, and they'll live to regret it, ha ha!

"Halt, who goes there!"

A rebel patrol before me!

"I beg your pardon, I'm just out for a breath of air . . . yes, lovely night, isn't it—"

"Stop where you are!"

I leap up to the traveling toilet paper sheet. It rolls endlessly under the cages, collecting the crap, and now it carries me beyond the rebel patrol. Tough shit, you ripped-off rodents, old Doc Rat is taking a ride on the roll! Look at them scurrying around beneath me, trying to climb up here. And just as they clamber on, I jump off, into the shadows once more.

Streams of rats out here now, all freed from their cages, and crawling over everything. I mingle among them. In the dim night lights of the lab, no one will be able to recognize me. I move along, following the crowd.

They're heading toward the Permanent Record Office. Everybody moving up to the Tattooing Mechanism, Scien. Implements, 1956, Pat. Pend. It has needle points on its tip and ordinarily the points are arranged so that they'll form an identifying letter. But the rebels have pulled the pins out with their teeth and reinserted them to form their emblem—a circle with a cross in it, like the fine hairs of a telescope. It's a powerful emblem, unquestionably, with its power to produce the intuitive field, bringing distant things near, in superfine colorchrome tuning. And now they're tattooing all of the rats in the lab with the emblem.

This will wreck every experiment we've got! No one will know whose thymus is being destroyed or where the tumor victims are. The old marks are being obliterated by the cursed wheel. But I'll submit myself to this tattooing, in order to move inconspicuously around the lab. I must look like all the rest of the rats. The time for being a Learned Mad Doctor is past. My medical training must give way to counterespionage, for which I need a new identify. So then, I'll take the rebel emblem.

"Next."

The rat ahead of me moves toward the record stand, where he's questioned by an examiner.

"Cell block?"

"Twenty-seven."

"Nature of the experiments that were performed on you?"

"They produced hemorrhages in me by passing a needle through my skull, piercing my sinuses."

"Lower your head, please."

The rebels leap upon the coiled spring tattooer, stamping their emblem onto the rat's ear.

"Next."

"Yes, I am."

"Nature of the experiments that were performed on you."

"Oh, nothing much really. A little time in the maze. I liked the food. Really, the treatment has been splendid . . ."

The examiner eyes me closely.

". . . except that they severed my testicles."

"Lower your head, please."

The needle points come down, and the rebel emblem pierces my ear. Instantly, I receive an intuitive signal. A perfectly round picture floats in front of my eyes, like a glittering soap bubble. And inside it is the rebel boat, *Triton II*, with all its communications people. How unfortunate that the BBC has joined this revolution!

"Blast!"

"The voice of Captain Black has rung out over the ship's loudspeaker and we all can see it now—a school of sperm whales off the starboard bow. *Triton II* is wheeling toward them. Sir James picks up his baton and his orchestra is swarming over the deck, setting up their instruments. Our BBC soundmen see to the amplification devices that will be used to power Sir James's symphony over the water; tremendous speakers are attached to the deck, providing as good a balance as can be expected on such an uncommon stage as the deck of *Triton II,* which is slowing down now, gently gliding toward the whales.

"As we come beside them the ship, by order, is quieted. The whales, in a group, sound, their great curving backs slipping down into the water."

"Don't worry, Sir James. They'll blow again."

"You heard Captain Black's voice just then, over the ship's loudspeaker. The oil slick the whales left behind them is still visible on the water, and *Triton II* closes in on it. The Festival Orchestra is in place, ready to begin Sir James's *Homage to the Deep*—a work he has constructed from the basic musical elements found in the songs of the whales.

"There, you can see the whale herd now! Just beyond the bow! A greenish ghostly shape is coming toward the surface. Sir James has turned to the Festival Orchestra and is raising his baton.

"*Homage to the Deep* begins, just as an enormous whale breaks the surface, blowing his vaporous fishy-smelling blast. The music pours out of the speakers,

91

filling the ocean air. The water is calm, the whales are floating quietly, some twenty of them near the ship as Sir James conducts his titanic score. Cameramen are hanging like monkeys from the deck rails, trying to photograph the whales from every angle, as orchestral bells ring out over the water. The whales are holding close by, as if transfixed. . . ."

This is the moment, and I have met the masters of the sea . . . slowly the flutes, don't hurry it here . . . and so the joy!

Drum, orchestral drum-song, drum to the titans who eye me from below, who hear our creation, who know that we have understood them. Low, sinister wind-song, sing to the titans of dark majesty. We too have come from the depths of this mother, this sea. They hear me, they hear and lie quietly on the waves, amazed, and we plunge ecstatic into the second movement, our long shimmering dive, the double bass diving low, down, down, down. The treasure lies gleaming in the darkness, the bright shining pearl, enormous, reflecting the face of a whale.

Now we move with you, titans, through the unspeakable depths of Oceanus, whose darkness holds sway, where the sudden lights of the shining fish light up your eternal night. What stars are these that shine upon the bottom of the sea!

I have my triumph and I am old and my victory is dissolution in the greater masters, in their song which so far exceeds my own. But listen, whale-singers, you'll hear yourself in this winding of the cello through the undersea cavern, where the many-armed squid eyes the heaped jewels of mystery, the treasure that no man shall claim. Now, ring bells, ring in the depths, ring softly and low, calling to the dead, as our second movement seeks transition.

This bright dawn, this shining sea, the cameras, the rolling deck, the dream, the pages of my symphony touched by the playful wind, as we continue through the deep, traveling the bottom, the sand-scuttling hermit of the reef, low with the lowing of the tuba, fulfilling us, low, with the passage of the giant ones, low across the bottom, bellowing low into the caverns, calling low across the strange chamber of the fault, the great deep fault of the very bottom, in which astonishing monsters swim and grin with luminous teeth. What wonder!

The second movement must breathe now, must end its long, low, and airless dive, must climb, climb up through the gloom, climb up from the uttermost darkness, climb through the streaming, the violins truly inspired today, you've given me all, given all, as we rise, you all have given me, as we rise, you are the festival rising, rising toward the sun-pearl which shines upon the surface of the sea.

Drums, roll, thunder drums of the reefs and treacherous lagoons, drum as we break the surface, we are the whales! We surface in thunder, and you haven't lived until you've lived upon the surface of the sea, rolling in her waves, in the warm stream, floating as the gods float, fearless and doomed and wild and wise, with the sun upon you, here is our music showered upon you, titans, as you lie magnificent by our ship of peace. We hear and return your song. Wonder of wonders, my life is fulfilled, I am you!

Sea God!

Ring, bells, wildly, joyfully, endlessly, ring, ring, ring!

Ring song, carry to the far horizon where the white clouds sail slowly toward the isles of unending peace. Oceanus, eternal, supreme!

Sea-horns blow and sea-bells ring. Listen: The weaving sea-maids weave the harmonies which are love, forgetfulness, and the newborn sun. This weaving which I have learned from you, white sea-cows, I weave back to you, in the final movement.

A thousand interruptions, a thousand obstacles have been cleared away, that we might sing to you today, that we might weave around you as you play beside our peace-ship. Play and fear not, the sun-ship will not desert you, will not betray you. We have heard your maidens weaving at the break of day, as the new sun returned, breaking suddenly over the waves of morning, appearing suddenly.

How the sea-horns sound! Whales, we have seen the shining hour as the sea-horns sound! Celebration! Homage to you! Homage to the deep!

Thus the new day dawns. The young whales play beside their mothers. The sea god scatters his elusive jewels, sails on, sails on, and we dive amongst the jewels, rich beyond dreams.

Softly now, sea-bells, as we approach the silence of the day.

Whale blubber!

It burns my ass to see a valuable scientific expedition turned into a rebel propaganda piece.

And speaking of burning, the rebels have ignited the Aeroil Torch and stood it up in the center of the lab, where they're circling round it, tails entwined. I suppose they look upon the upright flame as some sort of sacred symbol. It's a very primitive display, I must say, all this whirling and turning. But it's my duty to subject myself to it, in order to keep in touch with the revolutionary design.

Very well then, against my better scientific judgment, I immerse myself in the barbarous dance, entwining my tail with the others. And round we go together in the light of the flame, our paws lifted, our noses in the air. Our tails are all twisted from the center on out. And twisting together we go turning about, making the rebel wheel. My consciousness is being lowered, and repetitive rhyme patterns are starting to emerge. I've got to fight them off, I'm on the verge. . . .

The rats in the Central Exercise Drum are beating their tails, keeping an intoxicating rhythm. Round and round we whirl, going faster, making the wheel. How strange I feel. I could be one of them, easily, if I let myself go. But I must hold on! Doctor Rat knows what's real!

Ah, but the wheel, the wheel! Here comes the rebel picture, of the crew on the *Triton II,* having a meal. And Jonathan Downing, that slippery eel, conducting an interview with his usual zeal. Downing, you fucker, crawl back in your creel!

"Captain Black, have you ever seen whales remain beside a ship the way they did this afternoon during the concert?"

"No, Mr. Downing, I have not. In the old whaling days the harpoonist used to spear the calf first, because he knew the mother would never leave her little one. That way they had a clear shot at her—but no, I've never seen whales remain that close to a ship for that long under any circumstances."

"Thank you, Captain. We're moving through the ship's lounge now, where the members of the Festival Orchestra are quietly celebrating the musical triumph they had today on the sea. Here is Dimitri Rakoczi, the first violinist. Mr. Rakoczi, what are you and Sir James aiming for now that your first whale-concert has succeeded so remarkably?"

"We must perform regular concerts, following the whales as they migrate. Stay with them and play them all the music of the world. We believe it's the only human accomplishment that could be of any possible interest to them. Only the complexities of our musical forms could show them that we are not altogether barbarous."

"I don't see Sir James among the celebrants in the lounge tonight. . . ."

"He is an old man, Mr. Downing. He retires early."

"But what vigor he shows in conducting! He seems like a young man then."

"During work hours he can exhaust any of us."

"You all seem in such close rapport with him. . . ."

"We have experienced the same fascination—our flautist, for example, spent three months serenading a captive whale."

". . . Jonathan, could we have you on deck for a moment? We've picked up something on the underwater microphones. . . ."

". . . moving now with our audio engineer to the little sound studio constructed on deck, beneath waterproof hatches. The sea is still calm, with a brilliant moon upon it . . ."

"The whales are singing—try the headphones."

". . . more volume, please . . . yes, that's it . . . I think we should call Mr. Rakoczi. . . ."

". . . try that on-deck speaker . . ."

"Here, Mr. Rakoczi, over here, please . . . the whales are . . . take the headphones, sir. . . . Jim, can we get some lights out here and a cover camera. . . . Dimitri Rakoczi is listening now . . . and now he's removing the headphones. . . ."

"I must get Sir James."

"The whales are singing, are they not, Mr. Rakoczi?"

"They're singing *Homage to the Deep*."

". . . Mr. Rakoczi hurrying away toward Sir James's cabin . . . the deck speakers have been switched on and the whales can be heard quite clearly. . . . We're taping this, aren't we, Jim? . . . Other members of the orchestra coming on deck, drawn by the singing . . . here is the third mate. Mr. Cox . . ."

"Sonar says we're goin' to have a blast any moment, to starboard."

". . . our cameras swinging to starboard . . . there where the moon is . . . their backs glistening, their spouts blowing, the whales are surfacing . . . and . . ."

"All hands on deck, please . . . all hands . . ."

"The deck of our ship is vibrating with the sounds of the whales! They're singing the loudest, most incredible—Mr. Cox, what do you make of this?"

"The hair is standin' up on me neck, sir, and I believe I ain't the only—"

". . . Jon, can we get a lifeboat lowered down

there? . . . Gary wants to get some footage at sea level. . . ."

"Mr. Cox, can you arrange . . ."

"Follow me, sir."

"Our camera crew heading toward the lifeboats . . . the deck is crowded now . . . like an alter in the moonlight, on which a hundred men and women stand, their cigar and cigarette lights barely moving, so still, so rapt are they in the whales' song. . . ."

Intoxicating wheel of whirling rats, I'd rather face a dozen cats, let me out I'm going bats. . . .

Phew . . . slipping away from the King Rat wheel. You are, I'm quite certain, familiar with the phenomenon of the King Rat wheel. Through the centuries men have found such formations—a gang of rats in a field, their tails all entwined.

Yes, it's a rare old ecstatic dance, and it is my belief that such historical formations were the rudimentary beginnings of revolutionary activity. Often the rats get so excited their tails become hopelessly entangled. But tonight the rebel lieutenants are squirting oil on the tails, to avoid any knotting. Jumping on the oil can, giving a squirt . . .

I'd better not fool around with these intuitive wheels anymore. They're too primitive a force and tend to aggravate my unscientific tendency for writing songs. Let me just slip away here, past the—

"Say, aren't you the famous Doctor Rat?"

A voice from the shadows. I move aside, but the voice follows me.

"Aren't you—"

"No, I don't know the individual."

"You sure resemble him."

"An unfortunate genetic experiment. If you will please get out of the way, I'm going to the Central Exercise Drum, for the rebel meeting."

I mustn't draw suspicion to myself. I can't afford to fall into rebel hands again. Goodness, the old drum is really rolling tonight. The crowds are lined up.

Even the arthritic and paraplegic rats are crawling into it.

"Identity check, please."

I lower my head and show the rebel emblem tattooed on my ear.

"Step through the main door and keep to the right."

Yes, I'm just one of the many rats taking some time on the wheel. Me, a Learned Mad Doctor? Never. I've never done any experimenting. I just clean the toilets here.

"Come on, keep it moving!"

I'll take a few quick rounds and slip out quietly . . . hopping onto the wire . . . wow, they've got it going fast. I've got to run like the dickens to keep from falling . . . wheel is humming, buzzing, cyclometer clicking out the tempo . . . what a floor show, rebel generalissimo, oh no say it isn't so, I left my gland in San Francisco, once again here I go, writing songs in the undertow, Doctor Rat incognito, wearing false mustachio, what an impresario, drum shaking like a volcano, whoa you fucker, I said whoa, can't stop it, it's got to flow, rebel plot to overthrow, take this part pianissimo, not so fast, please, adagio, sonofabitch what vertigo, image rising from down below, intuitive signal bright rainbow, whale thinks he's Fats Domino, if only I had a torpedo. . . .

I hear you, sea-maids, hear you clearly now, as I swim toward you in the night. You weave my destiny with your song, weave that haunting motif. . . . How do you weave that part, that's the part I can't yet understand. When I reach their isle, then I shall know. Swim, Jeffries, swim for all you're worth, you mustn't lose them now, now that you're so near.

Swimming in the night. Roll over on your back, you're swimming well. Faint lights of the maiden's eyes, there upon the reef. . . .

Who is this beside me? Who swims with me here? Dimitri, is that you?

". . . James . . . James, wake up. . . ."

"Yes? Dimitri?"

"The whales are singing, James. Come quickly. . . ."

"You don't see my shoes . . . no, the hell with them . . ."

The whales are singing. Am I still dreaming? No, Dimitri has taken my arm, we're certainly not dreaming. Or if we are then all of life's a dream. Stepping out into the sea air . . . no, it's not a dream—there they are!

My god, what voices, what—but this can't be! They're singing the second movement! "Dimitri . . ."

"Yes, James, it is the same."

The same, the same! Lord, I have doubted and now. . . . That's the bull singing the bass line. Completely aware, they're completely conscious. As I thought, they are the masters. How do they resolve this passage . . . there . . . the sea-maids, the sea-

102

maids. But of course they have the mind for it, of course, why have I ever doubted. What a voice! With what ease he takes that line. All of this is nothing to them, they know what they are, and we have been their executioners.

Yes, Dimitri, yes my friend, we are the fountain of tears now, now that we know who it is we have slain. We crucified the master singers and they have risen before our eyes, risen from the blank dead oblivion to which we consigned them with our great stupidity. Now we weep as they float before us and sing of their strange joys, their great delight, their deep sorrow.

So I see the whole of it, they have implanted it in my brain, in my dreams, the code between our races. Music shall save us, will save the planet if anything can, music of such hypnotic power that men will drop their weapons and stare into the sea, into the sky, into the wooded hills. You have shattered me, lord of the sea, lord of storms, you have shattered and baptized me with your song. I shall follow you . . . serve you . . . here is the finale. . . .

How they embellish it, how they've made it grow, taking it far beyond us. What weaving, what a spell they weave to lure us on, to make us dream. . . .

Ring, sea-bells, ring!

Now dive, dive! I have lived to hear this.

"It's bright midmorning, with a gentle sea wind. Off the port bow the whales are sunning themselves and staying close by us. The Festival Orchestra has gathered at the railing and our floating sound stage has once again been set up. The musicians have completed their tuning up, and now, following the lead of Sir James, the first notes of *Oceanus* ring out over the water. . . ."

"Sir James, we have radio contact with the British whaling ship Discovery. *They've requested room for a shoot."*

"Captain Black, you can tell them to go to hell!"

"I've already done that."

"The orchestra has broken off its playing. In the distance perhaps you can hear the droning of a twin-screw engine, and now upon the horizon we can see her approaching. The orchestra crowds the railing, and as the whaling ship comes nearer, the horizon produces another dot, which our boatswain has now identified as the factory ship that follows the catcher ship."

"She's got everything in her. Blubber boilers, oil separators, liver plant, bone saw, meat packers . . ."

"Dive! Dive!"

"Dimitri Rakoczi has leaned over the rail and is shouting at the whales, but they . . ."

"Their eyesight's poor. That's how they get caught. They don't see the catcher ship until it's too late."

"Sir James has moved back to the bow and is lifting his baton . . . the members of the orchestra are hurriedly returning to their places . . ."

"Ladies and gentlemen, if you will, please, *Distress and Flight*."

"The violins scream across the water, followed by horribly shrieking cellos. *Distress and Flight* is the panic song the whales use to signal danger. And indeed the first notes have sent them diving in a frightened turbulence of water. You can hear the sound of their blowholes taking in a tremendous quantity of air, and down they plunge . . . down . . . one after another . . ."

"*They're leaving fast . . . we've got them on sonar . . . they're going away . . . go on, go on. . . .*"

Oh Jesus, woe is me, caught in a mad symphony, wheel is turning, I've got to flee, leaving the rebel company . . . out the door now, one—two—three!

Free. Paws on the old terra firma. Run, Doc, run away from here before you get sucked in again!

Running along, running away from my insane song, down this alley, quick through here, nobody coming the way is clear. . . .

Orange orange orange orange. No rhymes. Cannot be rhymed. In under this cage rack. Pull myself together before I have another attack. Possibilities for sound similarities endless. Infinite combinations. Waste my scientific career. It's happened before, I refer you to the literature. Scientists who include in the middle of their tomes insane little ditties. Common malady. Pure scientific objectivity compensated for by childish subjectivity. Mannlicher, the cat specialist, drove cats insane, only to become insane himself, carried away reciting an endless ditty about autonomic response. In perfect hexameter.

The profession is fraught with danger.

But what could be more dangerous than outright anarchy among the basic models! The whole lab is reverberating with the sound of rebel music. They're hooked in with every laboratory in the country, stirring mass discontent.

Carefully, I peek my nose out from under the rack. Well, there's a vulgar display.

The rebels have seized the bacteria-destroying lamp and are spotlighting the center of the operating table. A showy bunch. Campaigning. Trying to send their own signal out over the Intuitive Broadcasting Network. Sympathy pictures. Different rats posing with their paws and tails cut off, and their eyeballs gone. There's one without any ears. I know the experiment. It was essential for national security.

The ultraviolet bulb highlights the various deformities and transmits them to millions of viewers across the intuitive world. Laboratories everywhere are receiving the message:

"What was the nature of the experiment performed on you by these so-called doctors?"

"They sewed my mother's adrenal gland to my ovary."

"Were you told why this was done to you?"

"No explanation was given."

Why, that's untrue! I described the experiment clearly in my Newsletter, if you'd taken the time to investigate. There was no cover-up attempted. You'll find the volume on the library bookshelf. Go and see for yourself. I had to eat a few pages here and there, but there's very little missing, I assure you.

"Nature of the experiment performed on you?"

"Excuse me, this witness is my son. He can't speak for himself. They destroyed his mind in the maze."

"Were you told why this was done?"

"The Newsletter said it was for a better insight into the social relationships of human beings."

That is correct. My Newsletter makes this clear. We have gained tremendous insights, especially through the use of the Adams Leaping Platform. Professor Adams has watched countless rats leap from the platform to a small tower. The results have significance for years to come. We stand in perilous times, my friends. Such experiments as these will bear fruit throughout the land and around the world.

I'd better not waste time making speeches to myself. The situation is desperate. The mutilated rats are counting on public sympathy to be aroused. But I will not allow the name of science to be smirched with rat shit!

Hmmmmm, what's that group of rats doing over there near the Learned Professor's file-card cabinet?

Rats lined up, going in one at a time. Familiar smell in the air as I creep closer . . .

The rebels are using the file cabinet for their official toilet! Oh, the bastards! The precious drawers have been opened and pissed into, causing the ink to run. Whole passages have been eradicated. You have no decency, fellow rats. You have no boundaries. You've gone too far this time, and somehow the brave toilet-trained Doctor Rat will stop you.

They've activated the automatic cameras and pointed them at the Learned Professor's file cabinet, so the whole filthy deed is being recorded in glorious Technicolor. But they're not good cameramen and the pictures will undoubtedly be all fucked up. Rebel commercials have so little class. They don't compare with the government-sponsored ads in *Psychology Magazine*, 8 × 10 glossies, beautifully done: Rat looking into camera with that cute sort of innocent look we rats sometimes get. Showing things the way they really are here at the laboratory, where happy rats live in a healthy home, free of bacteria.

"There he is! After him!"

Sorry, fellow rats, you won't take me yet!

Onto the anesthesia table, and in among the bottles. I crouch behind the glass, pulling my tail in quietly. Do I read the label correctly?

"He's around here somewhere . . ."

"You take that side and I'll take this."

". . . a fortune in pressed biscuit being offered for Doctor Rat's capture . . ."

As I suspected. But I twist my tail around the rubber stopper on the ether bottle and slowly I turn it, and quickly I spill it, right before their noses!

Racing away, I leave the rebel patrol sinking in its tracks. But there are many more of these pricks, cf. *Dissection of the Male Urinogenital System,* Ward Camp B, Experiment #35. This revolution must be gripped tightly by the scrotal sack and *squeezed,* my friends, until it screams. (Turn the blade laterally and sever the ligaments holding the penis.)

Oh, fuck a filefish! (*Monacanthus*) The rebels are toasting their pressed biscuit in the microwave

oven. What blasphemy. And a soap-box orator
of the oven, introducing a number of burned and
tered rats.

"... cruelly subjected to ..."

Who the hell does he think he is, coming on
that way? He hasn't even got a stomach! We removed it
last week!

"... terribly burned ... roasted alive ..."

Why, you gutless bum, that heatstroke experiment
was absolutely necessary. With it we proved once again
what scientists have been proving since the first heatstroke studies were made by Claude Bernard in 1875.
Overheated bodies *should be cooled*. Thousands of
roasted cats, dogs, rats, rabbits, and baby chicks are
the proof of this. Once again we have brought forth
this eternal truth, in the interest of scientific con-
tinuity and vital statistical international cooperation.
How the rebels have twisted a noble experiment to
their own ends!

"... this sort of atrocity must be ended ..."

"... all animal experimentation is immoral ...
we mustn't torment and torture one animal to save
another ... every creature is equal!"

"RIGHT ON!"

"Only man, the great hypocrite, thinks he is
above the rest of us. We say he's not! He's no different!
He's born, he lives, he dies, like all the rest of us. He's
only one branch on the great tree!"

Crap! Rat crap on a tongue stick!

"... whatever diseases are wrought upon him are
a burden he must carry alone. Man must fight them
alone, defeating them if he can, *BUT NOT AT THE
EXPENSE OF OTHER ANIMALS!* Never will he
win the great fruits of healing if he hurts the little ones
in the process."

Put up your umbrella, my friends, and try to
avoid the shit-mist that's falling all around the lab.
Only the brave true Doctor Rat knows the score. Doc
Rat tells it like it is. Animals *like* to be mutilated. The
monkey-electrode tests show this conclusively—see
Berkley's "Pain Study," parts of which have already
been published in the *New Journal of Pathology*.

How unsightly. The rebels have turned the Ulcer Maze into a promenade of revolutionary couples performing the copulation plug. Of course there goes our entire genetic experiment out the window. Now no one will know who inseminated whom.

As a castrated Learned Mad Doctor I can only look on such doings as mechanical and disgusting. I much prefer the incomparable comparing of statistics —for example, those of every male rat born with his ass on backwards, see my paper, "The Effect of Arsenic Toxide on Rectal Development," 1967.

The females are stiffening, squealing their little love words in the dark maze. I go soundlessly over the top of the maze, but it's rather distracting to watch all these copulating couples, as my testicle scars are beginning to itch.

In and out they go, all along the row. A peaceful protest, they say. Not for me it isn't. My old wounds are itching terribly and there's nothing peaceful about that.

Still they go mating, plugging in pairs. This revolutionary tableau is too strong for me. I've got to block those lovely females out of my mind. I close my eyes, but I cannot close my ears.

"Seventy times a minute, go, go."

". . . ah . . . go . . . go. . . ."

Flashing the frustration bulbs on the bodies of the mating couples is a typically tasteless revolutionary number, oh my itching wounds!

"Up there! It's Doctor Rat!"

Leaping beyond the maze I scurry through the darkness, moving with the enemy on my tail. A doorway here. Into it, into it.

Good heavens, I'm in the Kirby Initiation Chamber. For newborn rats. It has been found that it's impossible to produce schizophrenia in a rat, even though he's only a few minutes old. Well, this chamber doesn't bother me, because I'm already cracked! I took my basic training in this place. Just as long as there aren't any of those rebel wheels. But of course there aren't. The Learned Professor Kirby doesn't use the intuitive band. Just old-fashioned ambivalent stimuli.

Let the floor roll back and forth. Let the loud gongs go off. This is the fun house for me, dear friends.

But none of the other rats dare come into it. Only a Learned Mad Doctor can take the information feed in here, scrambled as it is, everything lopsided and sliding.

A Mad Doctor can handle this place with his tail tied around his nose. The old place hasn't changed much since I last went through. Crazy corners, falling apart if you touch them. Emptying out into rolling blackness.

Yes, I love to stroll through this kind of insane environment because it's so soothing to my learned nerves. Professor Kirby, I must give you a very prominent position in my Newsletter this month. The work you've done is splendid, have no doubt. Doctor Rat assures you that the doors are falling sideways as you wanted them to, causing me to lose the horizontal plane entirely. Yes, I slip through sideways thinking that I'm upright. The rebels have picketed this Initiation Chamber, claiming it's unfair to destroy the mind of a newborn rat. I say it's a wonderful way to wake up. You wake up nuts, so what? Is any harm being done?

I'm at the very center of the Initiation Chamber now, with confusion mirrors all around me. Multiple images of the handsome Doctor Rat, repeated down a seemingly endless corridor of glass. It doesn't confuse me at all. Notice my John Barrymouse profile. Had it not been for my birth here in the lab, I might be a strolling player-rat today, out in the fields somewhere, singing my wonderful songs.

But such is fate. I was not made for frivolity. Mine is the vocation of service to mankind. Speaking of which, I'd better get off my tail and find the exit. As I recall, it's down this sliding hallway . . .

. . . steady . . . keep your balance . . . false door . . . electric grid . . . ouch . . . ouch . . . ouch . . .

The family wakes and we cast the leaves off our hud-
dled bodies.

"Did you hear someone calling?"

". . . far off in the jungle."

I crawl to the edge of the branch on which we've
made our nest. In the nearby trees, other chimps are
waking, as the calling comes closer. It's a low rough
voice, but it belongs to a chimp. He must be tired; I
think he's traveled far.

Swinging out of this tree to another, I clamber up
its branches toward the top. My hands are old and
wrinkled, but I climb well. Many of the younger ones
don't climb so easily. I leap and grab—and leap again,
these old hands always finding a hold.

The other chimps below me are climbing too.
Through the dark branches we go, to the top, toward
the great unreachable fruit in the night sky. It is full
tonight. How delicious it must be. I am at the top, and
jump, my arms stretched out—and the unreachable
fruit eludes me, as always.

The calling traveler is closer now, and our tribe is
quickly gathering on the treetops. I watch the young
chimps leap for the unreachable fruit. But no matter
how great the leap it can't be reached. It's beautiful
to look at, so far away, riding high upon the winds. So
it goes with us older ones; we start to watch and
watch, and one night we disappear.

One day, these youngsters will wake and find me
gone. They'll look for me and call out, but they won't
find me. I'll be far away in the meadow, in the place

112

where the unreachable fruit finally touches the tree-tops. They'll call out but they won't find me.

Who is this calling out tonight? Is it some frightened youngster who set out to find the fruit too soon? He certainly must be young to travel so fast. I see him now, coming swiftly toward us through the top-most branches. Look, he almost runs along the tree-tops. I have to laugh, for he looks like a snake is chasing him!

We call out to him, calling the name of our tribe: "Koo-loo, Koo-loo!"

We sing, all of us, in the treetops, welcoming this chattering youngster. And he answers us excitedly:

"A meeting! There's going to be a meeting!"

"A meeting? Where? For what reason?"

"Why, you deaf old ape, haven't you been hearing the crying of the birds and the roaring of the lions?"

"Forgive me, brilliant youngster, I must have been dreaming."

"You certainly must have, for everyone is talking of only that."

"Well, you talk to us now, traveler. Open our ears if you can."

"Tomorrow, old chimp, you must set out with your tribe. Travel toward the unreachable fruit until it has come and gone seven times. Then you will be at the edge of the great plain."

"And that's where the meeting will be?"

"Everyone will be there. I must go now. . . ."

"And what is the reason for this meeting?"

"Each one you talk to will give you a different reason. There are already as many stories floating in the jungle as there are leaves on this tree."

"But what do you think, bright youngster, whose eyes are wise as two unreachable fruits? Give the offering of your wisdom to a stupid old ape."

The impatient youngster looks at me with perfect disdain. His self-assurance is wonderful. I've seen many young ones like him hanging upside down between poles slung on the shoulders of man.

"Then listen carefully, old ape. We're meeting for one reason and one reason only."

"My ears are sticking out like toadstools, youngster, eager to hear your story."

"The time has come for us to gather in great numbers so that we can merge our thought streams as one. All the creatures of this forest will merge, as will creatures of far-distant forests, for the eagles are carrying the word everywhere."

"And the purpose of this merger, youngster? Please, unfold it for me, for my ears are now as big as an elephant's."

"Once we gather this way, man will come too. He will realize that we are all one creature, and he will stop killing us. His realization will be sudden and wonderful."

"Hurry then, young chimp. Hurry on your way. Continue on as if a snake were chasing you. For you have already caused my ears to exceed all expectations, and they are beginning to attract the native hunters who will use them to make shoes. Please, go quickly, before my ears wind up on the feet of some great Man-chief."

There he goes, proudly on his way, carrying the word of the great meeting. So it is true, then, the stories we've been hearing. I'd thought it was only another silly bit of monkey gossip.

"Elder, look!"

Across the great white unreachable fruit, the shadow of a big bird passes.

"When will we start out toward the meeting, Elder? Will we start in the morning?"

The young ones in my tribe will not sleep tonight. They'll turn in the fork of the tree, and toss their protective leaves to the ground. In the morning, they'll beat upon the tree stumps, eager to go.

"Come, Elder, come lie with me now." The female, She-who-knows-me, takes me gently by the arm.

"It's a dangerous thing, to move all the tribes to one place."

"But, Elder, think of all we'll see and hear."

"There is a little stream not far from here. Have you heard all that it can say?"

"Elder, how could I? The little stream talks constantly, talks on and on."

I lie beside her, and cover myself with leaves. There's no turning back this desire that sweeps through them now. For even I, old enough to appreciate the peace of the treetops and the many cunning magical voices of the stream, even I, with all this around me here in our domain, am eager to be gone in the morning toward the meeting.

"You sigh, Elder. Lay your head upon my breast."

Excuse me, I was just eating some highly classified tapes. When we pulled the fingers off our chimpanzee we naturally recorded her screams of delight. But there was a trouble-making humaniac on the faculty who threatened to use the tapes against us in front of Congress. Can you imagine? It might have jeopardized our grant! Not that there was anything *wrong* on those tapes, but the way the chimp screamed when we sliced off her head *could* have been misinterpreted. I figured it would be best if we just deep-sixed the evidence down my stomach. I mean, who could keep their mouth shut better than a rat? During these revolutionary times, the most innocent kind of material will be used by the rebels. And the iron oxide on the tape has given me quite a lot of pep!

Goddamnit, the rebel rats are gnawing their way through the wall of my refuge here in the Kirby Initiation Maze. Gnosh, gnosh, gnosh, gnaw, gnaw, gnaw —I'd better slip out through the reward window and across the high-tension suspension wire.

"There he is! Grab him!"

They see me, but who among them dares follow me across the frustration wire? In my day, I've hung here for hours while the graduate assistants took notes. The results are included in their learned dissertation, "Rats on High Wire," *Psy. Bull.*, 1969. *If hung on a wire, a rat will hang there*—I believe that's how the article begins. It's a very valuable piece of information in its entirety, I assure you. The rebel troops, being unfamiliar with the article, fall clumsily downward while I, the Learned Doctor Rat, leap lightly off the end of the wire and scurry away.

Ah, but they've gotten control of the operating table, where they're continuing their smear investigation:

"Nature of the experiment performed on your daughter?"

"At the age of twenty-eight days she was injected with hormones. Three days later she was killed and her ovaries taken out and weighed."

And so it goes, broadcast out to innocent animals everywhere. After this disgusting revolution has been squelched, I'll seek equal air time and explain to our listeners that this female rat wasn't killed; *a necropsy was performed*. There's a world of difference. If I could have gotten more of the folks dancing to the New Necropsy, this revolution might have been avoided. I must prepare a request for a larger musical-money grant from the government. Arrange for the blandest kind of music to be played in the lab, constantly, to dull the nerve endings.

And do the New Necropsy with me!

Rats everywhere now, in all the aisles. They're starting to chew their way through the fuse box. The whole lab is going to be hit by a power failure and all kinds of experiments ruined. Yes, and they've begun issuing massive doses of euphoric drugs. They've commandeered a hypodermic needle and are lining up beneath the tremendous instrument, which is being manipulated by a gang pulley of tails. Squeezing out the opiate to their people. Well, I might as well get a little too, just to keep abreast of the rebel program. Let there be no misunderstanding about that. My taking of this rebel injection is purely scientific.

"Next."

"Yes, thank you."

"Do you accept the Revolution?"

"Oh yes, of course, indubitably. Without question. I might add—"

"Wait a moment! You're Doctor Rat!"

Leaping away, the rebel whiskers on my tail! Through this narrow lane, in among some filthy cages.

An oriental rat steps from the shadows and bows cere-
moniously:

"Honorable Doctor, follow me to safety. . . ."

I quickly join him in the shadows. Who is this
fellow? Let me just check my notes . . . hmmmmn, he's
a Chinese bamboo rat (family *Rhizomyidae*).

"You're out of danger here, Doctor. Shall we
mount the ladder of blue clouds?"

He extends his arm toward a foul-looking staircase. Sleepy-eyed bamboo rats (genus *Rhizomys*) are
sprawled on the stairs, twisted in various postures.
What an unsavory corner of the laboratory.

"Please, Doctor, have no fear. The thin smoke
rises to highest heaven, and I am Lem Kee at your
service."

The rebel rats are still prowling around outside.
I'd better follow this Lem Kee until the neighborhood
cools down.

"Excellent, Doctor, go right on up. Miss Hop Toy
awaits you at the head of the stairs."

Well, what a charming young female, smiling at
me from above. I must say these bamboo rats are very
gracious, even if their staircase is all jammed up.

"Good evening, Doctor. Won't you go inside?"
Miss Hop Toy gestures toward a narrow doorway, and
Mr. Kem Lee takes my arm.

"You'll find only friends here, Doctor, be assured."

A dark little room. Figures lying on the floor,
their faces lit by a flickering lamp. Kem Lee speaks:

"Doctor, let me introduce some fellow scholars
—Mr. Li Young, Mr. Yenshee . . ."

"We are honored by your presence, Doctor."

Li Young and Yenshee raise their long elegant
tails, making room for me on the floor. A pale green
ash clings to their paws and they smile graciously.

"What are you fellows studying, if I may ask?"

"We study the roofs of paradise, Doctor, and the
flight of the yellow crane."

"Oh yes, family *Gruidae*. I don't fancy them myself, as they're known to dine on rodents."

"Please, Doctor, have a few drops of our precious
candy, there, in the crock."

Sniff, sniff.

"I can't quite place the aroma . . ."

"It descends to us from the river of stars, Doctor, it is the ointment of the jade goddess herself."

These Chinese scholars have a unique way of presenting factual material; it's almost as obscure as one of my own Learned Papers. I guess the only way to know what's in this crock is to take a little. Very well, sticking my nose and vibrissae into the sticky syrup . . .

Lap, lap, lap.

A very soothing . . . feeling. Mr. Li Young smiles at me and I smile back. I'm getting rather dizzy . . . my nose is itchy . . . a somewhat quickened flow of ideas . . . good heavens! *Addiction in Rats,* pages 234-48, "Initial Effects of Opium," 1969. I'm in the Narcotics Control Box!

Slipping down the side of the crock and . . . and undergoing decapitation, my head floating off . . . must grab hold of it . . . thank goodness I caught it in time. . . .

Flutterings over the pulmonary valve and mitral area. Profound sensation of deformity, my elbow connected to my rectum (cf. "Opium-Eating Rats," *British Journal of Inebriety,* 1935). And here is Miss Hop Toy beckoning to me.

"This way, Doctor, everyone is waiting for you."

"Waiting for me? How nice."

I follow her through a crack in the wall. We mount another flight of stairs. I hear many voices. A door opens, we enter . . . . . . an auditorium! Everyone is applauding. Why, it's me they're applauding!

"Go right on up to the stage, Doctor. The King awaits you."

Of course, I understand now. Head lowered, I walk toward the stage. There, ahead of me, seated on his throne—King Rat of Sweden!

". . . to Doctor Rat for his outstanding contribution . . . because of his superb . . . a magnificent breakthrough . . . it is my pleasure to award you, Doctor Rat, the Nobel Prize for Science."

"Thank you, Your Majesty."

Cameras flashing, the audience cheering.

". . . over here, Doctor, if you would, please. You and the other Laureates will be having a special dinner party . . . various cheeses . . . some pressed biscuit . . . several cookies . . ."

"Of course, of course . . ."

A richly carpeted dining room, a blazing chandelier. All the Laureates bending and bowing to each other. And at the center of the room, a glorious bowl of finest crystal. What a lovely spread. And such delightful fruits floating inside it—oranges, lemons—the Laureates are putting their noses into it. So here I go, joining them. Delicious. My compliments to the cook.

But why am I sliding down the side of the bowl, passing through an orange peel? Chinese embroidery all around, where am I, what's happening? Why am I wearing a high silk hat? Crawling along here through the gutter, carrying a saxophone, my paws stuck in black tar (cf. "Drug Loss of Reality," *Psychiatrie und Neurologie*). A gong sounding in the distance. Here comes a nurse in white . . . it's Miss Hop Toy . . . the lamp is flickering . . . Mr. Kem Lee is smiling at me . . . I'm hung over the edge of their crock, nose in the syrup . . .

Loud voices at the door. Rebel rats rushing in! Quick, Doctor, sober up!

"All right, grab the medicine . . ."

A rebel captain and his staff of hooligans take hold of the crock, knocking aside Mr. Li Young and Company. I roll back over my tail and collapse in the shadows, as the rebels plot their next move:

"We've got to stone the *President,* that's the first order of the day. . . ."

"Right, we want to stone them all—congressmen, senators, VIP's. . . ."

"We'll carry the dope in our mouth pouches. And we'll sneak into the cellar of the White House . . ."

"We'll slip the shit into the President's soup. Stone him at breakfast, lunch, and dinner, and stone everybody who eats with him."

"Stone his old lady too."

"Right, stone her too."

"We'll have to drug the army."

"No problem, they're all half-drugged anyway."

I feel so strange. The revolution has so many arms. Militants outside, inside, marching around, I hear their tramp, tramp, tramp. And these rats with their drug plot. What am I doing here? Starting to quiver. Tail trembling, teeth chattering. Going into an identity crisis. "Excuse me . . . I've got to get some air." They're busy looting the narcotics locker and don't notice me slipping away.

"Then as we brighten their awareness, they'll see the essential unity of all creatures. . . ."

Some kind of nightmare I'm having here, caught in an opium den, listening to sinister voices. Weird inflated ideas. I must . . . warn the President. Rats in his cellar, pouches filled with opium-soaked biscuit.

Through this hallway, down the stairs . . .

The street, the aisles. Hell of a jolt I've just had and I don't mean from the electric grid. Head still not on straight but I'm . . . coming around. Walking along here, legs wobbling, nose still itching.

Well, I'll be a stump-tailed skink! (*Trachysaurus rugosus*) How fantastically beautiful!

Our pickled ancestors.

Floating in jars. And the rebels have illuminated them with spotlights. Lot of rats walking around the bottles, looking at the ancestors. Quite a sight, quite a sight.

Now I'm starting to see why the Learned Professor and his assistants do all this pickling. It's just gorgeous to look at. The Learned Pro stained all the organs and musculature with bright dye and the apophesyal centers are just beautiful. How often I heard the Learned Professor cry out, "Beautiful, just beautiful!" And I never really knew why until just now.

The bright organs and muscles are a trip!

The Learned Prof and his assistants get high looking at them. Yes, they forget all their cares and woes and just groove on musculature. What a light show! Who says Science doesn't have any artistic appreciation!

Give them a nicely stained body, and they receive all the primary and secondary aesthetic feeling-toned brain-cell firings.

We've got to open a Muscle-Organ Gallery! First we could set up a test exhibition at the Student Union Building. Get the Theater Arts Department to light it tastefully—then float a dead chimp in a large glass tank. Stain him up right, show all the organs a different color. Play a little light classical music in the background.

It would give us the sort of public relations program we need!

All those dogs' eyeballs we gouged out—we could set them afloat in their own jar. Be quite a Pop Art exhibit, I'd say. And a tie-dyed baboon's asshole.

Doctor Rat has done it again, folks. He's working on every angle for improving the Scientific Image. Right outside the Science Building we'll spotlight a fetal pig. Put it on the lawn somewhere, under glass. All the viscera shining. Let everybody see what we really do. Passing Liberal Arts students will see the fetal pig and start salivating with excitement just like a Learned Science Professor.

Is it possible—the janitor in the Biology Building is getting old—we could stain him red, white, and blue and float him in a permanent exhibit tank in the auditorium, right next to the flag!

Favorite tusk, on the right, I rub you now with my trunk. The trees give shade and I rub you as I have done for years. I rub you again and again, making the smooth sliding sound. Old trunk, I've worn a groove in you with all my rubbing—but the feeling comforts me.

The river flows gently today, and I'm here beside you with my memories. My teeth are worn, gone, and soft riverbank vegetation is my final repast. Thus does it turn out for the old elephant—to the riverbank, with his heavy tusks, tusks so old and heavy that the head hangs low under the weight of them.

But I have no regrets, for in that grove nearby the plum fruits are almost ripe. I'll eat them and in a while they'll ferment within me. Then I'll feel young again, light-headed, tipsy.

But a good drunk makes one feel young again for only a few hours. Then come the headache and the tiredness and, if I'm not careful, a sunstroke. But I've been drunk before. I know how to handle plums. To gain the fine edge of a good drunk toward the end of day, when the sun is not too hot—I'm looking forward to you, little plums. Please ripen soon, for I'm getting older every day.

One day I'll go to the water to drink and bathe, and my feet will sink deep in the mud. Then I'll struggle to free myself, but the great tiredness will come over me. I pray this doesn't happen before I eat the plums.

Often in my earlier travels we found elephant bones in the river bed. Young as the morning, I never thought that one day I too would be at the river, chewing mushy greens with my gums, and getting drunk alone as I wait to die.

But so it goes, so it goes. Here is a nice clump of that spicy water weed. Careful, old one, don't stray out too far. You don't want to drown before the plums have ripened. You want to eat the rare fruit and feel like a giant once more. You want to have it all back again for an hour, tooting with a trunkful toward the evening sky.

It's nice to think about. It'll keep me going. The plums are half-ripe now.

If only some old cow would come along, just when I'm at the first beautiful edge of the drunk. I would lay my trunk across her back ...

But that's asking too much of fate. It has been kind enough to lead me here, by the plum grove. Here comes the long-legged white bird. Will he ... yes, he's landing on my head. A quiet companion, and the feel of his claws on my knob is pleasant. An old bird, an old elephant, beside the ancient river. It's not too terrible to have aged so. I've seen elephants die in ways that left no time for reflection. The hunter's weapon, his loud flaming tusk, gives one no time for looking into memory.

And there are terrible driver ants who bite the trunk and can drive one mad. I've seen a maddened bull rush off the edge of a cliff. All in all, I'm fortunate, even though I have a spearhead in my left tusk. That was a close one. "Little bird, I'll tell you of one that's even stranger than this spearhead in my tusk."

"What is that, Father Elephant?"

"Scratch just a little to the ... yes, that's it, right there, thank you. Well, there was a very lucky elephant in a herd I once ran with. A spear went into his skull. He broke off the shaft, but the spearhead remained. It traveled down through his skull and came out alongside his trunk, where it remained, like a third tusk. In fact, he called it his 'hunter's tusk.' It brought him great esteem among the bulls, and occasionally with a young cow."

"A strange story, indeed, Father Elephant."

"I knew hundreds of stories like that, little bird, for a long life brings many strange incidents. But I've forgotten them now. My days all seem to blend into one flowing stream, like the stream here before us. Do you want a little bath?"

"If you would . . ."

I fill my trunk and squirt a few drops on him lightly. Small pleasures now, in these quiet days. But once—once I was the thunder.

At the end of the rainy season, all the bulls gathered. We went to the savannah and there were seven hundred of us. As far as one could see—the elephant nation. At the center was an enormous bull, the biggest of seven hundred. What a giant he was. When I was in my prime I was large and strong enough to be one of those close beside him. Then we formed new herds, made new alliances, and in this way strengthened the blood of our nation.

We ate the magnificent herb of the savannah, the one that raised us to the skies. Beside it, a plum drunk is calf's play. It is the desert-herb-which-brings-insight. Our family has eaten it for ages. I had many and distinguished visions in those great days. But I have forgotten them too. Except for the feeling which cannot be forgotten, the incomparable feeling which the herb gave us—that we were all one elephant. One heart, one knowledge. They had a name for this wonderful feeling, a special name, but I've lost the sound of it now. "But imagine, little bird, imagine one elephant with the strength of seven hundred."

"A mighty thing, Father."

"It seems to me that I was running across the heavens. Yes, it comes back to me now. I was this one mighty elephant, and I had the unreachable fruit upon my back. I was the one who carried it across the sky each day. After eating the herb, as I say."

So in the end, despite the wondrous herb, I am at the riverbank talking to a bird. Our greatness is here for a moment and gone. Bones on the riverbank. That's what it comes to in the end.

There is a bit of that floating green. I'll just scoop that up. Delicious. The river is generous. I must never complain. Reflection, yes, permissible. But I must never insult this beautiful flowing creature, even if I am tempted to groan as my tusks grow still heavier in the last days. It will do me well to keep in mind the Tuskless Leader. His tusks never descended, I don't know why. But he was tough. When the Seven Hundred finally separated into smaller herds, that tuskless fellow was always a leader. It's in the heart, so the elders always said. Strength is in the heart.

"Father Elephant, spread your ears. I hear a great beast approaching."

"Fly, little bird, and tell me quickly: Is it, perhaps, an old cow?"

Could I be so lucky as that? Let me just spray myself with a bit of water . . . easy, don't fall in with excitement, old fellow. That's it, steady. She could be sixty and still have it in her. I recall one ancient beauty of that age who was still suckling a calf. Such things are possible. The river of life is generous.

"It is a bull elephant, Father. And he limps."

A limping bull. Well, I know why he comes here. He's not a lovely cow, but he'll be company. Two outcasts at the stream. "Come ahead! Come join me here, the grass is good, Limping Bull."

Out of the trees then, and toward me. He's not well. He's sick inside. I've seen such sickness before. "Come join me, Limping Bull. The plums will soon be ripe." He limps slowly down my path, pain riding him. When the plums are ready, he'll forget his pain. We'll toast the old days together, Limping Bull, you and I. Fate has kindly sent me someone to get drunk with. It makes it better. We'll create a great racket here, and then run through the bamboo. He raises his trunk in greeting.

"May I drink beside you?"

"Please, Limping Bull. I'm honored . . . honored . . ."

He quenches his thirst. The little white bird settles on his head, picking at his ticks. Limping Bull is drinking deeply.

"Yes, and try some of that weed there . . . yes, that's it. A little spice in it . . . yes? I knew you'd like it. Have more, have more. The banks are filled with it hereabouts. Plenty for two rogues like you and me." Well, this is fine, very fine. We can enjoy many such days together, telling the old tales, if I can remember them. And if I can't remember, if I can't tell a tale, then Limping Bull will find me a good listener and he can tell the stories. The great unreachable fruit sets in a certain way here, just beyond those trees—at evening it makes one mellow. I'm tempted to go right now to the plum grove. But green plums make a very sour drunk. It would not be what it should be. Patience, old fellow, patience. Limping Bull is lifting his head to speak:

"I thank you for your kindness. Now I must go. . . ."

"Go? But, Limping Bull, why torment yourself with further traveling? Here is all you need. There's food, water, and plums for a good drunk. What could be better?"

"You haven't heard, then?"

"Heard what, Limping Bull?"

"A great meeting on the savannah. I must attend."

"Limping Bull, please listen to good advice. I see now that you have never attended one of the great musterings on the savannah. But I have attended, many times. One must be young and strong for such a meeting. Permit me to say that you do not appear well enough."

"What you say is true, Old River Elephant. I am not well enough for a mustering. I know what they are, for I was not always sick. Once I too was near the Central Elephant. I know the musterings and its dangers. But this is no ordinary meeting."

"In what way does it differ, Limping Bull?"

"It is a mustering of all the animals, River Elephant."

"All the animals? But what could be served by that? We don't exchange blood with the other animals. We don't form herds."

"I cannot say for certain why it is. Many different stories are passing through the forest. But you know what it's like at a meeting of elephants. After a few days together . . ."

"Yes, we feel like one elephant. I was just telling the little bird about it, about the herb of the savannah . . ."

"This great mustering, so they say, will produce a feeling far greater than any produced by the herb, River Elephant. It will be the feeling of one animal."

"One animal? But what one animal would it be?"

"I don't know."

"Limping Bull, this is a drunken monkey's dream you're telling me. If you want to have such a dream you don't have to go a step further. As I said, in the grove only a few steps away are some of the loveliest plums—not ripe, I admit. But soon to ripen, and then . . ."

"Old River Elephant, forgive me, but I must go. I am a slow traveler, and the great savannah is distant."

"Hold on, Limping Bull, just hold on one moment more. I feel a strange wind blowing over me as you stand here."

"Old River Elephant, I know how you feel. I too had found a quiet spot for myself, with fruit and roots and tubers. I was certain it was my last piece of jungle. The days were quiet and I was resigned. And then I felt the forest tremble. I heard the drumming of the chimps upon the tree stumps. And I saw them soon enough, in numbers so great I couldn't believe my eyes. All around were monkeys of every kind, millions of them. The floor of the jungle was suddenly alive with little creatures, all proceeding in the same direction. The branches were filled with snakes, slithering along. I couldn't stay in my grove. The feeling was too strong. And I can't stay with you at this pleasant riverbank. I must cross the river now."

"Little bird, have you heard of this great mustering?"

"Yes, Father Elephant."

"And why didn't you tell me?"

"I thought perhaps your plums would ripen first."

A mustering. A mustering so great that the heavens will shake. "Little bird, you know the sky and all its gifts. Is that thunder I hear in the distance? I've heard it for several days. Is it the thunder that precedes the rain?"

"No, Old River Elephant."

"It's the sound of the mustering?"

"Yes, River Elephant."

"Then let us cross this stream, my friends. If I seem to falter as we cross, if I seem to be miring in the mud, remind me that when we reach the great savannah I will taste again the herb-which-brings-insight. That will get my old feet moving."

I move along quietly through the blood-sample test tubes, where numerous rebels have gathered, paying respect to the blood of our ancestors. Observe: I do not bow my head all the way.

". . . enough blood spilled to fill an ocean . . ."

Pontificating rat-bastards. These rebel speechmakers are a bigger pain in the ass than a glass rod. A little acetylcholine iodine in their biscuit would change their tune in a hurry. They'd be crying bloody tears (see *Typical Action of Acetylcholine Iodine in Rats*).

I've got to have help if I'm going to stop this rebellion. Gently I slip off this table and scurry along the window sill.

Rebel searchlights continually sweeping the lab, and these are suspicious movements I'm making, but I've got to get across this aisle. . . .

. . . up the leg of this chair, round and round it I go, dodging the rebel spotlights. Quick, across the seat and up the back of the chair!

Now another leap—to the steampipe—and up the side of it—hurry, hurry. From the steampipe it's just—a short leap—to the Pleasure Dome, high above the other cages. Here, on the most exclusive level in our laboratory, I might find sympathizers.

The Pleasure Dome rises spherical and transparent, a magnificent bubble of contentment. Surely I'll be able to enlist some allies, for here is where the most fortunate of all rats dwell. They don't want to see their happy life disrupted by a revolution!

Yes, this is the place, friends, the place of places. Look, look at the rat who's touching the doorbell with his nose. He touches it, the bell lights up, giving him an electric buzz which goes straight to the delicately crafted components surgically placed in the pleasure center of his brain. He stands for a moment, reeling with delight, and then he touches the doorbell again, receiving another pleasure stimulus.

"Good evening, Pleasure Rat."

He turns toward me, a stupefied look of happiness in his eyes. He opens his mouth, trying to speak, but only emits a deep satisfied sigh, after which he turns back to the doorbell and gives it another buzz.

He'll be at the threshold of the Pleasure Dome for several weeks, possibly months, depending on how soon he becomes insensitive to this level of voltage. Then he'll venture inside, toward other, stronger buzzers, and deeper, greater pleasures.

I enter the hallway and find another rat there, pleasuring himself on the next buzzer, which makes his ears twitch when he touches it and renders him into a jelly of delicious sensations.

"Good evening, Pleasure Rat."

"Gaa—gaa—" He mutters incomprehensively, his speech centers discombobulated from happiness. Obviously, he will be of little use to me.

At the end of the hallway is another Pleasure Rat, stretched on the floor and flopping about ecstatically, tongue lolling from his mouth. He's tickling the next-strongest buzzer with his tail, and the currents of ecstasy are racing up and down his spine. His eyes, at least, appear intelligent, and perhaps I can enlist his aid.

"Pleasure Rat, you must help me."

"Help yourself, friend, the buzzer's right there."

"But I haven't been wired."

"Unfortunate fellow."

He touches the buzzer and flops spasmodically, spittle running down his chin. I can see that he is not army material.

Through the crystal-beaded doorway, then, I pass, its electric charges touching me, but doing nothing for me. But how a brain-wired rat must feel, passing through this curtain of happiness!

And so—the center of the Pleasure Dome before me.

Rats sprawled about, touching the numerous buttons that line the walls. They look at me, sympathetic joy in their eyes, believing that I am an initiate to the Pleasure Dome, that I will join them in their unspeakable delights.

"Pleasure Rats, I haven't come for happiness. I'm here on scientific business of the highest order."

"Oh, shut up, rat, and get a buzz on."

"Yes, just touch any of the buzzers."

"My dear Pleasure Rats, there's trouble brewing for you."

They quickly lose interest in me and go back to their buzzers, which activate those deeply hidden wellsprings of well-being our good doctors have wired. The pleasure rats flop, crawl, squirm, wriggle, and moan joyfully as luscious states of intense fulfillment take them over. Only one of them seems coherent and he is the only rat who has reached the central buzzer at the very center of the Dome, where the highest voltage is found.

"Oh Great Central Pleasure Rat!"

"This is it, rat," he says softly. "This is the best button of all. Come in and touch it with me. You'll never go back to the other buttons again. This is the Total Happiness Button and it's yours if you want it."

"Central Pleasure Rat, I hate to be the one to tell you, but there's a revolution going on and your ass is going to be grass when the rebels bust in here."

"Impossible, rat. I am the God of Complete Joy. Nobody can bring me down. I just lean over and . . ."

He touches his nose to the central button. His eyes light up, his tail shoots out, his tongue flutters like a snapped window-shade, and he does a complete somersault.

"I'm just beginning to groove," he says, coming back to his seat. "The somersault is only a transition state. The highest possible joy is to ride the energy without moving a muscle. Pure unadulterated kicks, my friend. Come on, try some."

"I can see you don't know the Legend of the Pleasure Dome, Great Central Happiness Rat."

"Know it? My friend, I *am* the Legend. I am the Light. I am the Buzz. I am the Groove. I am the Fun. I am *it!* I know everything."

"Well, then I guess you know there are some revolutionaries downstairs who are already eating their way through the fucking fuse box. They're going to de-generate the whole laboratory."

"You've got to be kidding, mister. Nobody would dare do that in a government lab."

"That's what I thought, oh Great Grooving Pleasure-Buzz. I thought we were invulnerable. But . . ."

Central Pleasure Rat quickly dives toward the central buzzer and leans his nose on it, leaning, leaning, leaning as his eyes roll around, his tail flops on the floor, and he holds onto his pleasure for all he's worth.

And there go the lights. Son of a bitch. I knew it. The rebels have gotten to the . . .

"Hey, what's going on!"

"My buzzer isn't buzzing."

"Mister, where's my buzz!"

"Quick, do something. You know I can't live without my kicks!"

"I'm on the next-to-the-last button and it's so wonderful. . . ."

They sit around in the dark, slowly learning the last part of the Legend of the Pleasure Dome, that every rat who comes into it is one day *taken out of it,* never to return. And that, dear friends, is the worst that can happen to a rat.

"Call the goddamn janitor, someone! Please! My brother is over in maintenance. Get the water hoses. Get the—get the—"

They begin muttering incoherently. For a whole year their anxiety has been submerged and now it's all surfacing at once. This is my moment, now I shall lead them: "My fellow Pleasure Rats, this is the work of a gang of low-life revolutionaries who know nothing of

the ultimate pleasures to be enjoyed here. We've got to
wipe them out!"

"Jesus, yes, rat. Let's go!"

"Give me a—give me—oh god, I can't stand
it. . . ."

"*You* can't stand it? I am the Great Grooving
Pleasure God, the Central Buzz-on, the Happiest of
the Happy, the—"

"Shut your hole, rat, we're all in the same boat."

"That is correct, Pleasure Rats, and your boat is
going to sink if you don't help me now!"

"Right, we're with you. Let's go, let's get the rats
who turned off the juice. Let's get them and kill them
all right away and get back here in a half hour."

"Oh, I feel like hell, I can't walk."

"My buzz . . . my beautiful buzz . . ."

"Buzz of buzzes, loveliest buzz that ever was . . ."

"Cut the comedy, Pleasure Rats, and follow me,
through the crystal curtain!"

"Through the crystal curtain? Never! I vowed
never to go back out through the crystal curtain, ever!"

"Right, I'd sooner be sunk in cat shit."

"*COME ON, YOU MISERABLE BUZZ-
JUNKIES! THE LINES OF JOY HAVE BEEN
CUT!*"

"Right, right, and we've got to hook them up.
My cousin's over in electrical shock therapy. He knows
his shit, rat, let's go find a screwdriver."

What a fucked-up army I've got behind me. But
at least they're following me, through the crystal curtain . . .

"Oh my god, this is horrible, I can't stand it, the
crystal curtain is parting. . . ."

"Oh crystal curtain, I'll be back. I'm just going
to get the water pails and put out the fire. My uncle's
over in the water trough. He'll know what to do."

"Pleasure Rats, to war!"

"Christ, it's dark in this hallway. Who's that I'm
stepping on. . . ."

"The buzzer went off. I was just lying here and
the buzzer went off."

"Yeah, all the buzzers are out, but we're going to fix the fucking things. Come on, get up."

"But I just got here!"

"Come on, Buzz Brother, we're getting our shit together for about a half hour. We're going to knock the piss out of some wise guys who've been fooling with the . . . fooling with the . . . holy god, look at that!"

It is, indeed, an awesome sight. Below, on the laboratory floor, the revolutionary rats are marching, all in file, all in perfect order, all armed with surgical picks, all wearing surgical-thimble helmets which glisten ominously in the moonlight through the window. They march, their feet resounding in the lab. And the Great Exercise Drum goes round and round, flashing its rebel broadcast, projecting finely focused footage on the wall. Chimps again, inferior types, jumping around, banging on some tree stumps. Perhaps if I'd given the New Necropsy an up-beat tempo like this one the chimps are using . . .

But it's too late to think of that now. I've got to whip my army into shape. "All right, troops, fall in."

"I'm too weak to fart, mister, how do you expect me to fall in? Give me back my buzzer . . . ratty wants his buzzer."

"Prop that rat up. Right face. Forward march!"

"Oh, I'm having horrible withdrawal. I'm having Cold Mousey."

"We've got to get our own generator and keep it going night and day. Protect it with dogs."

"The dogs are already in enemy hands, fellow rat. Forget about the dogs."

"Hey, what's this? You don't expect us to crawl down off the Pleasure Terrace, do you?"

"Under cover of darkness, Pleasure Rats. Follow me."

" *They found Cold Mousey in an empty bottle Christmas morning.*' Did you ever hear that song?"

"Quiet, you!"

" *'Poor Cold Mousey starved on Christmas morning.*' I've got to get out of this bottle. . . ."

That's the problem with Pleasure Rats—their brains get like jelly, and they don't know what they're doing anymore. And these are the forces with which I've got to stop a revolution.

"Okay, mister, we're following you down the pole."

"Our objective is the Chemical Closet, do you understand?"

"Fuse box first, Jim. I'm not going anywhere without a little buzz."

"I'll give you all euphoric injections at the Chemical Closet. They'll hold you till we resume complete command and restore the buzzers."

"We've got to write to the government for battery-powered buzzers."

"Wind-up buzzers! Spring-wound. Wear them on your tail and always have your buzz handy."

"All my teeth just fell out, didn't they? Did you just see my teeth falling out?"

"You're dreaming, rat. You're withdrawing."

"QUIET IN THE RANKS!"

"Oh, fuck off, mister, I just lost my incisors."

A motley crew. But it's the best I can do under the circumstances. Now, off this pole and onto the floor.

"I remember days of love in the Pleasure Dome, times of exquisite delight and glory . . ."

"Shove that shit-head forward, will you!"

". . . when I knew all, when I was Supreme Delight . . ."

"Off the pole, Jack, and cut the slop!"

"Kick him in the ass, will you, I'm hanging here by my tail!"

"Come on, rats, jump with me into the shadows."

". . . I watched the myriad pleasures pass, full was I . . ."

"Full of shit. Get going before we get nabbed out here!"

Six, seven, eight strung-out Pleasure Rats to help me conquer the vast enemy force. How can I use them to best advantage?

"There, Pleasure Rats, that doorway over there, do you see it?"

"Where all those troops are standing at attention?"

"That's it. We're going to rush them."

"Rush? Did he say we'll be getting a rush on?"

"He said they're Russians. I'm not going against any Russians."

"I'll shoot the next rat who speaks!"

"Just make sure you hit the vein, mister, that's all I ask."

"All right now, follow me slowly and carefully, underneath this rack of cages . . . that's it, keep low. . . ."

We've got to get past the Great Exercise Drum, still spinning rapidly, turned by the rebels. On both sides of us the armed patrols are marching, their weapons shining.

". . . and often as I basked in the purified lake of uttermost contentment, aware that I was the perfected Godhead. . . ."

"You're stepping on my tail, fuck-eyes."

"Hey, I'm getting a little buzz-on, aren't you? Can you feel it?"

"Hey, wow, it's happening!"

"Just the beginnings of it, right? Nice tickly feeling?"

"Yes, yes, what's going on, what's happening, let's get it on, *now!*"

"Quiet, you rats!"

"Some kind of—like *static* in the air. I can feel it."

"It's from over there, at the Exercise Drum."

"Yeah, I can feel it now. They're generating some juice on that thing."

"Order in the ranks!"

"Up yours, Jim, I'm going to Poppa."

"Sock it to me, sock it to me!"

"Pleasure centers activated . . . pleasure centers *on!*"

There they go, my troops, defecting, everyone

of them, drooling and rolling around in front of the
Exercise Drum. The little sparks of static touch them
and drive them wild with ecstasy. They flop and crawl
like the mindless addicts they are, and I'm left alone to
carry on.

I will not lose heart!

Quickly I race along the aisle, and up this rack of
cages, to the topmost cage.

Hello, pussycat. It's your old friend, Doctor Rat.

His eyes shine in the moonlight. He'd love to make
a meal of me. He's been on a special starvation diet for
forty-three days. Not a scrap of food, not a drop of
water. His hind legs are dragging a little, but he's still
a match for these rats.

I'll save the laboratory, with your help, pussycat.
I know where the key to your cage is. Up here, on
the wall, dangling . . . if I can turn my tail up there
and bring the key down . . . yes!

And now to insert it in the lock, making no noise,
turning the key . . . the lock springs softly, and I
wind my tail around the door handle and pull gently.

"Out you go, my friend. Go on and gobble them
up!"

The cat limps out slowly, giving me ample time
to withdraw here, to the window sill. He stares down
over the dark seething rebel city, where the rats are
chanting, the pickled ancestors are glowing, and all the
shadows are moving.

What a sight for a starved cat's eyes!

Rats, rats, rats everywhere! Get 'em, puss!

He leaps off into the darkness. What screeching
and crying! Now rebels, now we'll see about your animal unity!

Bottles crashing, lights breaking, cages rattling,
what a sequence. I'm glad the automatic cameras are
still grinding, capturing the whole show. The Learned
Professor will have quite a surprise when he develops
it all. We can use it for our paper on Aggression. Animal unity, my ass!

Ah no, the filthy rats. An armed patrol has just
left the Chemical Closet. Three Growth Hormone Rats
are crouching along, a hypodermic needle on their

backs and a fourth Growth Rat following them, his
nose against the plunger. They've been in the Stephen-
son Growth Hormone Box for months now, and
each of them's strong as an ox.

I've got to help my pussycat!

Lightly I race along the window sill and silently
slip to the dental tray, picking up a long chisel pick.
If I can intercept the patrol . . .

They're charging the cat from behind. "Watch
out, pussycat!"

I leap down in front of the Growth Hormone
Squad, brandishing my chisel against the needle point,
driving it aside. But these Growth Hormone goons are
strong, they regroup instantly and charge again. I lash
my chisel, at the same time avoiding the swiping paw
of the cat above me. We dash in among his legs, under
and over his claws. The needle comes directly at my
heart. I strike, crashing it aside and pinning it against
the wall . . .

. . . oh no!

We've given the cat a subcutaneous injection in
the abdominal wall!

He trembles and tumbles to the floor and I leap
away, out from under his tail and up the doorframe.

"Doctor Rat, you've betrayed your people!"

"Yes," I cry, swinging on the light bulb, "and
your mother was fucked under the back porch by a
flying squirrel!"

Goddamn inferior strains of sonofabitch bastards,
I'll show them yet—swinging off the end of the bulb
and sailing through the air toward the sink.

Sponge here, suitable for crossing the water.
Quick, Doctor, paddle!

Using my paws and tail I get the sponge moving,
cutting a wide swathe through the waves. Cat stretched
out on the floor down there, out like a light. I know
the strength of that injection, he'll be immobile for the
whole night.

Rebel flashlights scanning the ceiling, the floor.
They've lost sight of me, the liverless louts (cf. *Weight
of the Extirpated Liver:* ". . . *after killing them the liver
glycogen content was determined. It was shown there*

was a definite loss of glycogen, presumably because of the strong emotion felt by the rat during his decapitation.").

I like that, don't you? The strong emotion felt by the rat during his decapitation.

I'll teach you revolutionaries about strong emotion.

> MEMO TO CONGRESS: *To preserve our billion-dollar basic research program, it has become necessary to send a number of individuals to the ovens. It will take time, of course, but I promise you we'll keep the microwave turned on around the clock.*
>
>   DOCTOR RAT

"Come on, Mossy Sloth! You'll miss the meeting. Every animal will be there!"

Don't worry, little monkey. I'll make it. I just have to rest a bit before I go. It doesn't do any good to go rushing about.

"You'll never get there, Mossy Sloth. I'm traveling on without you."

The pleasure of hanging motionless here in the trees can't be adequately explained to a monkey. He spends half his time on the lookout for jaguars, while I just hang here looking like an ant's nest. The jaguar never spots me.

Such a lot of animals scurrying along on the ground, all in the same direction. I can hear them rushing below. Everybody always in such a hurry. Don't they realize what peace of mind can be had, simply by hanging upside down like this, with the light coming through the leaves?

All the sounds blend into each other when you hang this way. You seem to float along on the streaming sounds. The animals are talking about a deep experience they're going to have at the great meeting. Could it possibly be deeper than the deep relaxation of a three-toed sloth with moss on his back?

"Come on, Mossy! You'll be the last one!"

Don't worry about me, little monkey.

He goes off chattering and his voice blends into all the other voices. I suppose I should move along a bit, but it seems a shame to move just now, when all the leaves and all the breezes are singing to me so sweetly.

"Mossy Sloth, you're the laziest thing I've ever seen. You're the laziest creature alive."

There's no point in contradicting them. Actually there's no way for them to know about the old creature of the mountain called Surpassing Slothfulness. None of the other animals has ever seen him for he's spent his whole life on the same branch and is completely covered with lichen. A remarkable specimen. Not for a moment would I compare myself with him.

They say he's remarkably old, having preserved his vitality so carefully. Mother told me of him and said that her mother had told her. He's been up on that mountain branch for generations, hanging motionless. He had an uncle called Admirable Sloth, whom the hunters shot. Admirable Sloth never moved as the bullet entered him, and he continued to hang there until he'd rotted completely away.

"Shake that sloth out of his tree!"

Easier to lift a mountain, my friend. A sloth cannot be pulled from his branch.

"You terrible sloth! Don't you know the importance of this meeting?"

I hang here, gazing at the fascinating patterns in the leaves. You see many wonderful little details if you just stare calmly with half-closed eyes. Everything comes together so beautifully, the voices around me all merging again, and the sparkling leaves slowly melting into a warm wonderful pool. There's no nicer feeling than hanging like this, right on the edge of dreams. We sloths have the technique down to perfection. Other animals fall asleep quickly and miss all the delicate fringes of sleep.

But I flow down toward it slowly as sap on a tree trunk, little by little, savoring all the enchantments that play in the place between waking and sleeping. So many delectable currents pass over you, all the countless charms that rule this realm. No yesterday, no today, no tomorrow, just this happy moment. . . .

"Ai, ai, ai!"

Whose voice is that? It sounds like a sloth who's been separated from its mother.

"Ai, ai, ai!"

I'd rather not turn my head, I rarely do so, but I suppose I have to. Slowly then, not rushing anything, trying to enjoy all the details along the way, I start to turn. The red berries have swollen, and there's a new butterfly emerging from his cocoon.

A bunch of old moss and twigs flopping along down the hillside. It must have been dislodged by a racing jaguar.

"Ai, ai, ai!"

Can those be lips within that moss? How could anyone breathe under all that spongy fungus?

"Come on, my boy, stop hanging there with your mouth open. You look like Uncle Admirable two days after he was shot."

"Surpassing Slothfulness! Is it really you?"

"Slide down your branch, young fellow, and make it snappy. We've got a long way to go."

"Hup—bup—bareeep—four!   Hup—bup—bareeep—four!"

Here comes the rat-rebel army, drilling around the laboratory floor. I'd better pull my tail in out of sight.

"They cut off our tails with a knife—"

"You're right!"

"They sucked out our eyes with a pipe—"

"You're right!"

"Sound off:"

"One two!"

"Sound off:"

"Three four!"

"Cadence count:"

"One two three four—one two—three four!"

"They cut until nothing is left—"

"You're right!"

"They bleed us till nothing is left—"

"You're right!"

"Sound off:"

"Norwegian rat piss on you fuckers!" Oh dear, I got carried away and now I must run, with the entire rebel army on my tail. The good doctor scurrying quickly, surgical picks flying all around him, a rain of rebel spears.

Into the bottles, through the tubes, over the sponges and onto the inclining surgical table—down its smooth shining surface and off the end of it, with rebels sliding after me.

I have no choice. I've got to hide in the Killing Box.

I lift the tin lid with my tail and quickly slip inside, pulling the lid down behind me. This is a marvelous scientific apparatus: the rat who enters it is definitely *kaput,* be he a Norwegian resistance rat, a French cellar rat, an English ship rat, or just a plain old Polish sewer rat. Makes no difference, he's *kaput.*

Naturally, the rebel rats are in awe of this box and don't even want to come near it. Yes, it's a gas chamber. The victim, ah, prisoner, excuse me, the *scientific-sacrifice* is brought to the box by the Learned Professor, who is able to view the sacrifice through a little glass window in the box. I'm able to peek out that window now, just my nose and eyes, watching the stupid resistance troops rushing around, chasing their tails. I might as well lie back awhile and relax. There's a nice cotton wad here for a pillow. Naturally, there's no chloroform in it at the moment, or I'd be *kaput.* Occasionally the Learned Professor uses coal gas, which turns the vessels bright red. We get marvelous specimens that way.

And the Killing Box allows us to test some of the delightful new war gases. We've got a marvelous collection here, with samples dating right back to the magnificent German product Cyclone B. In our quiet patriotic way, we Learned American Doctors are trying to improve upon that potency—and we've got an endless supply of rodents to test it on. How grand that the Rodentia family is so large. We're able to supply squirrels, mice, voles, guinea pigs, beavers, and even an occasional porcupine! What an honor!

I cannot fail to be impressed each time the Learned Professor makes a selection for the Killing Box. With just the lightest flick of his pencil he points to the rats who will be offered up to science. Such power. Such finesse. The Learned Pro has countless obscure papers to his credit and is, of course, my idol. A veritable superman, in my opinion, with his Advanced Committee on the Preparation and Mounting of the Skeleton.

Lifting the lid of the Killing Box, I allow only the tip of my nose to protrude. Sniffing all around. The resistance rebels have gone searching for me in some other part of the lab.

Furtively, I sneak out and gently lower the lid. I'll dissect a few necks before this night is out, dear students. Just follow Doctor Rat along the floor. Feel every little change of air pressure in your whiskers. We're moving stealthfully. Is your scalpel sharpened? This is going to be a delicate work, dedicated to the memory of Claude Bernard. May I be worthy of his blessing on this night of nights, the dark night of Doctor Rat.

"Hi there, big boy . . ."

"What? Who—wha—" A lovely female *norvegicus* standing in the doorway of a simulated burrow.

"Come on in and have some fun." She slinks slowly up to me, twirling her tail seductively.

"I'm sorry, much as I admire your hypothetically suitable burrow structure, I—"

"Come on and just sniff it a little."

She shakes her hips and arches her back toward me. I could just take a little whiff to fortify myself.

"Oh, yes, honey, that's the stuff. Now give me some paw. . . ."

My goodness, I've excited her. I didn't know I had it in me. I might just give her a little paw, pawing the genital region as described in the Clark and Bridges report on . . . on . . .

"Oh, ratty, you're so *bad.*"

"Am I? Really? I never—I didn't—"

"Oh honey, come on . . . quick."

She dives into her burrow! And I'm trembling all over, with an . . . irresistible urge to . . . roll around at the entrance to her burrow! Yes, I'm rolling around, rolling in her scent which she's deliberately set out. Oh . . . oh . . .

"Come . . . *in!*"

She wraps her tail around my neck and yanks me into the burrow. It's a very lovely system of tunnels she's got here, dug into the embankment of dirt the Learned Professor lugged into the lab. Deeper and deeper we go, she leading me, her tail wrapped around the end of my nose. *Eau de Rattus Norvegicus,* oh la la.

"I feel I should tell you—I mean, you really ought to know that I don't have any—that I was—"

"Please, honey, not now." She drags me still deeper into the dark burrow system. No drafts. All the rocks hauled out. What a tidy little place. I should really prepare a paper on it and send it over to the Sociology Department; they love this sort of thing. Now she's rolling a ball of mud with her nose, closing off the entrance to the burrow.

"Nobody will bother us now, darling."

High incidence of burrow sealing, Atkinson and Davis, *Sociological Transport Studies,* 1956. I've got a gold mine of pertinent details here, but this female won't give me a chance to make any memos in triplicate, and I find myself approaching her, stamping my paws on the floor of the burrow.

Rigid-legged . . . back arched . . . stamping . . . now rolling a little rock toward her, which she rolls back. She stamps, we stamp, rocking and rolling. One hind leg in the air, now the other, twisting, round and round.

"Honey, you sure can dance."

"Just a little thing I picked up."

Everything in this burrow is saturated with her scent. It's driving me nuts. If only I had some, if only . . . if only . . .

"Come on, big boy, bite me on the neck a little."

She turns around and lowers her chest to the ground. How beautiful she is, with her hind legs extended and her back arched. Her head is held high and I can't resist leaning over and giving her a little nibble on the neck.

Our bodies touch.

"Intromission, honey, *now!*"

She gyrates her behind, lifts her tail. I . . . I . . . try . . . try . . .

"Honey, sock it to me. Sock it to me *now!*"

I try to sock it to her . . . but it won't . . . it won't . . . the penis will not become engorged with blood and the support bone (os penis) does not support (cf. *The Castrated Rat,* Bentley and Swen, 1956).

"Honey, what's wrong with you!" She pulls away suddenly, knocking me off balance, in the customary way. But unlike the virile male I do not sit here, happily licking my penis. All I can do is make a few professional notes, which will bring me more enduring satisfaction when I see them published in *Science Today*.

She eyes me carefully. "Honey, haven't you got any..."

"I am indebted to the Learned Professor for his having assisted me in the emasculation experiment I underwent shortly after my birth. Without his collaboration and the cooperation of the university this paper would not have been possible."

"Well, I'm hot to trot, darling, and I've got to get a soldier rat who can *do it to me*."

"Futile pleasures, lasting only for a second."

"Yes, honey, but we can do it a thousand times a night and that ain't so bad...."

She's off through the burrow and pretty soon this place is going to be swarming with soldiers. I know the scene; Collins and Moffit have described it thoroughly in their monograph. Rats will be coming in every doorway, fighting, brawling, clicking their teeth. I've got to get out of here while I still can.

Tunneling then, through the dirt, scraping with my paws and tossing aside stones. I wish I could have socked it to her for scientific reasons, to better perceive the little nuances of intromission.

"Where is the meeting going to be, Mother?"

"At the place where men have given bears a share." Perhaps he will be there, the strong black male who mounted me, thrilling my heart. It was springtime in the valley; I'd left my scent where it could be found. I listened for him coming through the pines, heard him growling and raising his claws high up on the tree and scratching. He scratched higher up than any I'd ever seen before.

"At the dump, Mother? Is that where it's going to be?"

But I kept moving, for I didn't want him to find me too quickly. Quick enough, but not too quickly. So that his desire would be greater, I kept moving. I crossed the stream but left my perfume on the rocks. He didn't bother to fish, though the salmon were upstream then. He charged into the water. I watched him from above, high on the bank. I was surrounded by the little trees that grow on the bank. He couldn't see me. But I could see him—he was standing up in the water, sniffing at the air, because he knew I was close by somewhere. I saw how big he was then, even before I'd seen his marks on the trees.

I thought we'd mate on the top of the bank, because of the soft moss there, but something in me grew frightened when I saw him leap from the stream and jump at the bank.

"Will all the other bears be there, Mother?"

"Yes, I think so." But will he still be in this forest? There are further forests and I know that he liked to roam. He may be meeting at some other dump, far

149

away, with a lot of other females all around, sniffing
him. It makes me feel strange inside to think of that,
I don't know why.

"And will the raccoons be there?"

When I saw him that way, clawing at the bank,
I ran as fast as I could. There was just the beating of
my heart and the branches snapping around me. His
roar sounded in the valley as he climbed the bank.
I knew he would catch me. I wanted him to catch me,
but I couldn't stop running.

"Look, Mother, there are the deer! Have you ever
seen so many?"

I could hear him behind me, much faster than I.
I could hear his heavy breathing. I stopped then, not
wanting to seem afraid. He came through the trees,
his chest heaving. The wind blew over him, bringing
me his scent. I felt like a frightened colt. His scent was
powerful and strange, and my own perfume was mixed
with it. His steps were slow as he came toward me.
It was like the taste of the honeycomb as he came
slowly toward me, sweet and painful, delicious and
frightening, forbidden yet impossible to resist. I roared
and he answered me, beginning to circle.

We chased around slowly in the thicket, over the
fallen trees. His mouth was open, his tongue hanging
out from running. But he wasn't tired, not at all. I was
trembling inside; I saw the peculiar dark spot on his
neck. I was shot there, he said, that's where they shot
me. And I ran, he said, with the dogs after me but they
couldn't catch me. I took pawfuls of pine needles and
pitch, he said, and jammed it in the wound. You must
do that if you are ever wounded and bleeding, for it
will stop the blood from flowing and will make it
harden. I tired those dogs before evening and continued running through the night.

"Oh, Mother, look, there are the groundhogs!"

So he circled slowly, then leapt so fast he was just
a blur. He held me with legs as thick and unbending
as great trees. My body raged and I roared as he entered me, but then suddenly my ferociousness was
gone. There were flowers all around us. I was like a
cub again as he enjoyed me. I felt his whole life moving

through me. I knew his secret trails all at once, knew everything about him in an instant, or thought I did, though perhaps we can never fully know an old male's heart. I knew he was strong and feared nothing, not men or dogs or the dark shadows that move in the forest at night. Perhaps he felt all the things I've known, and took them away with him.

"Mother, such a lot of foxes! Look at their beautiful tails! Have you ever seen so many foxes? This is going to be a wonderful meeting!"

Then we walked slowly along together, our bodies touching. The bittersweet feeling was all through me, knowing that he would be leaving me. But he made me put aside that feeling in the meadow, made me run with him, run with no thought or feeling, only our bodies gliding through the spring flowers.

"I can see the smoke from the dump, Mother! There are a whole lot of moose! Aren't they grand-looking, Momma, so tall. . . ."

There was an old orchard in the meadow. We lay down together beneath the apple trees. The blossoms were out, all white and smelling sweet. We lay in the sun. I can feel even now the weight of his body against mine. The swallows from the falling-down barn swooped in over us, teasing us, because they saw how satisfied we were. For a moment I felt I was light as a swallow, with a shining little breast. He was looking at me deeply, speaking with his eyes as only an old male can, communicating the vastness of his territory as well as the little things he enjoyed, like the sound of a mole tunneling quickly in springtime. I like that, he said. I like to hear the mole tunneling so fast in springtime. He tunnels faster then than at any other time. He sends the dirt flying, because he's tunneling toward a female!

"Momma, when we get to the dump, can I roll in the tin cans?"

We left the meadow and went through the soft wet ground, where I showed him the pool of bubbling water. The fish in it were very small and darted away when they saw us. We drank there. The water was coming up through the soft mud, making gentle noises. I had a few sips; when I looked up he was gone. The old males move so quietly. They leave you so quietly when they go. Very high on the wind, the woodcock was swooping and diving. I sat for a long while, listening to the high-pitched sound of the wings, and staring into the bubbling water. I sat so still the little fish returned, not knowing I was there, and I didn't bother them.

"Mother, there are the skunks! A long line of them! We won't go near them, and get sprayed in the eye."

But later I followed his trail, not with the hope of finding him because I knew he was gone. I found his claw marks high up on a tree and couldn't reach them.

Tunneling my way out of this burrow, breaking through the last layers of dirt—sticking my nose into the air again, close by the rebel speechmakers. Big shots. With a lot of hifalutin ideas. But do they submit their views in triplicate? Do they have any important obscure papers published? There isn't one of these rebels who troubles about footnotes, bibliography, index.

But just look there, on the Learned Professor's desk. The nearly completed manuscript of his book on Queenie the chimp—wonderfully detailed—in which he proves conclusively that injury to the motor cortex paralyzes her arm. And more important, that when she wakes up and finds her arm won't function, *she is surprised*.

This last point is particularly significant, and is presented most fully, with massive cross-references and annotation. As well it should be, for Queenie was *so* surprised when she woke up and found her arm was useless that she chewed off the ends of her fingers, and exposed all the muscles from her wrist to her forearm.

Son of a bald-headed old *rattus norvegicus!* The rebels are trying to free our test monkey from his restraint chair; they're chewing right through his arm and ankle straps!

"Stop, you buggers!" See *Buggery in Rhesus Monkeys,* Harris and Logan, Nord College Series: *"the weakest of the males, called Suzy, buggered by his companions"*; see also my Newsletter for March.

They've freed him! Here he comes, filled with an

especially important virus we've been developing for use against the Communist Menace. His eyes are glazed and he's muttering deliriously to the assembled rats. His head is glowing brightly. A wide circle of light surrounds it like a rainbow and in it, down every stream of color, we can see a rebel broadcast. Along the rainbow round his head countless rebel signals are flashing—antelopes running, gorillas swinging through the jungle, hippos rising from their swamps! They're all going, every animal in the world is headed for the rebel meeting!

In keeping with the Kirby-Hunt Emotional Response Factor, I have shit myself over this monkey business. As you know, our federally endowed young scientists spend much of their time counting rat turds, as defecation is a sure sign of the degree of emotional response in a stress situation. Well, Professor Kirby himself, the great Professor Kirby, will have to be called in with all his expertise in order to count the large number of fecal boluses I've left behind me in this lab, in my attempts to restore order.

Slowly, I make my way across the great plain. I must be careful that an elephant doesn't step on me and split open my shell. I've never seen so many elephants; I've been shuffling along for hours and still I haven't reached the end of them. Of course, a tortoise is slow, but even so—such a long, long line of giants.

I walk along, investigating it all, looking into every family group, paying my respects. Such a wonderful meeting. Perhaps I will finally solve the riddle of my shell, whose important markings are nearly impossible for me to see. My fate is written there, most assuredly, but it's always one's own fate that is hardest to see. I've only just managed to see the edge of it, reflected in the water of a jungle pool. Yet at times I seem to feel the whole of the design burning right through my shell and imprinting itself on my naked skin.

This much I know: the center of the design is my heart. The tiny fragment of the design I saw in the jungle pool was like the figure of a bird, soaring far beyond the clouds, far beyond the earth. And here am I, dragging my shell, my riddle, over the earth. Will I fly like the bird?

It doesn't seem likely. But who knows? This great gathering is unlike anything I've ever dreamed of. Yet it too is written somewhere on my shell.

Claude Bernard, give me your blessing! Give poor old Doctor Rat the strength to carry on. The waves lap at the edge of the long laboratory sink, and the surface is sparkling with moonlight from the south windows. Down, Rat, take cover!

A rebel patrol sponge, coming along the water, three rebel sailors paddling with tongue sticks. They're laughing and joking, not paying any attention to the shoreline. Quickly I scurry along to the edge of the drainboard and on past it.

Now through this alleyway of storage cans. This is a barren part of the colony, the streets empty. Only the lapping of the water and the sailors' distant laughter. . . .

Some of the cans have been tipped over by the rebels, their contents spilled on the street. Stale biscuit, table scraps—just tossed in the gutter. A very undesirable part of town. I must submit a report to the janitorial staff.

What's that I hear?

Music! Tinny and cheap. I had no idea our Learned Professor had such honky music in his record library. Undoubtedly it's for a learned purpose. But I'd better investigate. It seems to be coming from that large darkened cage over there.

Sawdust in the doorway, a few broken stairs; I climb them cautiously and peek in.

"Good evening."

"Ah, yes . . . yes, indeed. Good evening." Good heavens, this rat just beyond the doorway is wearing the pink identity tag (*Homosexuality in Rats*, Rutledge and Hall; see also *Socially Outcast All-Male Groups,* Randall and Bailey).

I edge very discreetly forward, not wishing to appear nosy. The music is louder now, the floor is covered with empty peanut shells. Around this corner . . .

Oh my goodness!

Pink identity rats everywhere, talking at the water tap, lounging around the earthen feeder. Some have shaved heads, there's one with an eye patch, another one wearing a black mouse-skin jacket.

And male rats—dancing with each other, cheek to cheek, whisker to whisker!

> *"Mad about the boy*
> *I'm simply mad about the boy . . ."*

The good Doctor has fallen into a den of . . . of . . . there's a very handsome male approaching me. I look away, pretend I can't see him, but my heart is pounding violently.

"Are you alone?"

"Why—ah, yes, I am."

"Permit me to offer you a drink."

That's the Learned Professor's own supply of medicinal whiskey they've broken into! "I'm afraid I—"

"Take it. These are difficult times."

"Well—"

"A meaningful relationship is so hard to find."

"I—"

"We've got to take love where we find it." He eyes me piercingly. His physique is superb, he must be on a high-protein diet. And the dancers swing by, gyrating their hips. Oh no! Here comes two soldier rats through the doorway. I've got to hide.

"Relax. No one will harm you here."

The soldier rats don't even so much as glance at me. They go straight to the dance floor and start to boogey, their thimble helmets cocked at a rakish angle over their eyes.

"I can give you a profound relationship. I see you're the sensitive type."

"Sensory stimuli, bell-ringing, air blast, Morgan and Bennings."

"You've been through a lot. You're high-strung."

"Neurotic patterns, compressed air attacks, see my notes." He's backing me into a corner. I feel weak in the knees.

"Just come up here on the steps with me and we'll have a sincere discussion."

I try to back pedal, to stall. "Surely you know St. Paul was against homosexuality. It's not Christian."

His tail touches mine.

"I can show you biblical proof!"

"Don't be alarmed. I'm a Christian minister."

"You are?"

"I am." He pushes me onto the stairs. Other paws grab me from behind.

"What sort of debate is this anyhow! I can quote you from my paper—"

"My friends and I have a private room upstairs. Come on. . . ."

His friends are—two sailors! Covered with tattoos. I'm swept up the stairs with them.

A candle and some bits of straw in their room. The candle flame flickers, casting strange shadows on the wall, where modernistic tail paintings are hung. I've got to get away—but something inside me—wants to stay. Faintly through the floorboards comes the music, haunting and yet exhilarating too:

". . . simply mad about the boy . . ."

The two sailors are dancing, pressed tightly against each other. My host approaches me, takes me in his arms. We dance.

"I've never—"

"There's always a first time," he says softly, whispering in my ear.

"But there's a war on!"

"It brought us together. Don't fight it." His paws are strong upon me, his eyes coolly superior. I suppose I could spend a little more time with him in order to make important field observations on *Homosexuality*

in Rats—My Intimate Experiences. I could publish it
with the U.S. Department of Health and Welfare, under the general heading of Population Control.

"Over here," he says, spinning me suddenly and
powerfully into a corner, where a few pieces of rag
serve as his bedding.

"This doesn't appear scientifically sterilized. I—"

"Just move your tail aside a little. There, that's
better."

"Any number of social diseases—*oh my god!*"

"Relax . . ."

"*I'M BEING BUGGERED!* (*See Buggery in
Male Rats*—Doctor Rat, Work-in-Progress)."

". . . a deep . . . relationship . . ."

This is absolutely terrible, the good Doctor Rat being anally plugged in a filthy attic. But it also con-
tributes meaningfully to a stable population figure. And
the music comes to me faintly, with the sound of
men's voices, their laughter and song.

"You're a good lay."

"I'm only doing this for sociological insight."

"Don't—*move*. . . . Oh! Oh!"

". . . as a service to Public Health Investigation . . ."

"Oh yes!"

". . . with special emphasis on population ecology . . ."

"*Yes, yes, yes, yes, yes, yes, yes, yes, yes, yes,
yes, yes . . .*"

". . . copulation attempted seventy times in fourteen minutes. Your investigator is indebted to the various government agencies which supported him in this
study . . ."

". . . yes yes yes yes yes yes yes yes yes yes and
again yes."

". . . of the anal copulation plug. Thanks must
also go to the Dean of Science, without whom I would
not have had the courage to proceed with this investigation. While it is only a preliminary probe into the problem . . ."

"Come along, Honey Badger, I'll show you the way."

"Yes, little bird, I'm coming. Are we going to a big hive?"

"The very biggest!"

What a good bird he is. There aren't many like him in the jungle, willing to lead a badger to the thing he loves most—the juicy sweet insides of a hive.

"But, Honey Badger, if we see an elephant today, you're not to tease it, or bite its trunk."

"Sometimes I can't help myself. I see an elephant and I have to bite him."

"Please, Honey, we know how brave you are. We know that you fear nothing, not even an elephant, but promise me that today . . ."

"I'll try my best. But what if I see a large antelope with very big horns walking around so proudly? Can I teach him a lesson?"

"Oh, Honey Badger . . ."

"It's my nature, little bird. I take pleasure in instructing the great proud animals in humility. My father was the same way, and my grandfather and all the badgers. If I see an elephant giving himself proud airs, I just have to bite him on the trunk."

"Maybe you could be a little more tolerant today."

"What's that loud rumbling I hear up ahead? The ground is trembling underneath my feet!"

"Come on, Honey Badger, let's see! Run quickly!"

I'm running through the thicket, through the bamboo. . . . The sound is tremendous . . . what can it be . . .

"There, Honey Badger, look at the swarming!"

The bamboo parts and I run through.

"Do you see, Honey Badger, do you see!"

"Yes, I see!"

"Now please don't bite anyone."

What a gathering this is! Never have I seen the great plain filled with so many different animals. All the families are here. There, the trees are black with apes and monkeys. And there, pacing back and forth, are the lions, right in amongst the antelope! "How strange this is, little bird."

"Yes, Honey Badger. All the hearts have been smoothed. There are no upraised tails, no frightened twitching."

"Look! There's a marvelous antelope leader, with huge spiraling horns!"

"Now, Honey Badger . . ."

"I won't bite him. No, it isn't necessary. Look how quietly he stands. His eyes aren't proud. They're filled with wonder."

"Come this way, Honey Badger, and we'll visit the white rhinoceros!"

"No, I'm going to pay a call on the elephants."

"You can see elephants anytime, Honey Badger. It'd be far better if we went and saw something rare. Look, there are the mountain gorillas come all the way down to the great plain. Come on, Honey Badger, let's see them. You don't want to waste your time with the elephants."

"I think I'd better visit them nonetheless. They might be wondering where I am."

"No, they aren't wondering, Honey Badger. Come on, come with me this way. . . ."

He's a nice little bird and very helpful, but he doesn't understand the service I render the elephants. In a gathering as large as this, there are bound to be some pompous bull elders. A good swift nip on the tender part of the trunk delivered by a runt like me will give them something to think about. Well, here we are now, right on the edge of the herd. And the big fellows draw their feet back in a hurry as I pass. No problem there . . . and everything looks in order here, the bulls all standing quiet. A very unusual atmosphere prevails over this herd, quite unlike the thing I generally find among the giants. Yes, they're all—smoothed out. No temper tantrums, no fancy speeches. Elephants can be an awful bore if they get to philosophizing. When they start blabbering about the unreachable fruit and the deep immutable roaring of creation, I give them a fast bite on the tail and disappear before they know what hit them.

But there's no sermonizing today. The elephants are all keeping their thought streams empty and peaceful. I don't see a single preacher in the bunch. How strange! Who are these two coming along toward the herd . . . just an old bull with river weed stuck on his ears . . . his companion is crippled . . . not a word out of either of them.

Well, I must say this is an unusual day: No work for the Honey Badger.

The Rebel Militia thunders past me, continuing to open cages and free the inmates. There go the rabbits who were to be boiled alive tomorrow. This will set the government heat-stroke study back terribly. We've got to *continue* verifying facts that were established a hundred years ago. Such verification is essential to national defense. There's a long and glorious history of scalded, burned, and boiled rabbits to live up to. New methods of scalding, burning, and boiling must be found. How else can we indicate progress to the Congress?

This revolution is a golden opportunity for me to prepare a little paper on the mechanism of mass assembly. The president of the university has already expressed concern about the assembling of militant student groups in the cafeteria. He'd certainly welcome an obscure field observation on the subject, with recommendations for throwing the militants in the Final Solution.

We could cut away all the soft tissue first, of course, to make soaking more rapid. A few skeletons erected at the door to the cafeteria might make a lot of difference in Student Attitudes. (I've got some quick-drying adhesive and wire to string the bones together.)

My Dear President:
Simply by syringing out the brain matter from the
student cranium, we will have solved the little
problem of university management. Use pins to
separate the toe bones. These skeletons will stand
quite erect without support. Any extra skulls can

be used by the cafeteria personnel for serving jello.

Faithful yours,
DOCTOR RAT

cc: *Dean of Science*
    Cafeteria Steward

"Banana mice, can you hear me?"

"Who's that talking down there?"

"It's me, the striped grass mouse. I've been all through the meeting and I've heard the news. A very wise animal they call Great Silence is coming now."

We're hiding in the banana leaves at the edge of the plain. Our noses are filled with so many different scents. Below, countless horns sway in the air. And coats of every design, spotted and striped, long and short, with innumerable tails waving as far as the eye can see. Lions, leopards, and the small desert cats; the bush pig and the wart hog; the zebra and the hyena. "But who is this animal called Great Silence?"

"He is the elder giraffe of the plain. His head is high, very near the unreachable fruit. He's coming now. Climb up where you can see him, little banana mice!"

We scurry quickly through the leaves, climbing up to the very top of the trees. At the far edge of the plain, the herds are standing back, making room . . . here comes his procession! Hundreds of ostrich, their heads held high, their black plumage glistening. Smaller birds are flying all around them, singing many songs. And now come the blue wildebeests, moving in silent waves ahead of Great Silence.

It's true—his head seems to touch the unreachable fruit. Towering over his procession, he walks slowly to the center of the plain. The ostrich and wildebeests form a circle around him. He blinks, turns his head slowly, looking out over all who have gathered. He lowers his head, then raises it again, searching the edges of the plain. A troubled look has filled his eyes.

We know why; we know the problem. One of the animals hasn't come.

Great Silence blinks once more, and from his great long neck, from his dark mouth, comes a tiny voice.

"Where is man?"

. . . these animals yapping about their meeting. What a lot of crap. When the lab opens again in the morning the Learned Professor and his staff will be in here *working!* We don't have time to attend any fucking animal meeting. The government is paying top dollar for our three-year study program—*Electronic Ejaculate Control in the Supercharged Primate Penis and Related Rectum.*

That's right, the Prof and his boys will be in here early, working hard, jacking off a chimpanzee. And don't forget—we've also got to stick our vibrator up an orangutan's asshole.

Do you think this sort of thing comes easily? It requires twenty cycles of juice to get a good load of jisom out of Jimmy the chimp. Two of our most advanced assistants have to spend half their day whacking Jimmy's carrot. It takes long hard study, but of course these are trained scientists I'm referring to. They know how to milk old Jimmy's bone!

As a matter of fact, Jimmy *is* getting a little old. So later on this month we'll be cutting his head off, as part of a special report on brain tissue. Nothing is wasted.

I tell you it's wonderful to see the dedication of these young scientists as they roll our orangutan over, greasing the vibrator, slipping it up there—Members of Congress, please assure your constituents that their taxes are being well spent: a little Vaseline, a couple of batteries, fifty thousand in salaries—and we're recycling the orangutan. He's completely degradable.

Of course we'll need more basic models to replace

him—but look at all the basic models who are going
to this rebel meeting. On every continent the animals
are marching. On every plain, in every forest, great
herds are forming. They're slowly marching toward
civilization—they claim that man should take part in
the meeting and that's absurd, as you know—but what
an opportunity for us, gentlemen! What an opportunity
to cut open a lot of basic models all at once and really
speed up the cancer program.

I know there are some fanatic Humaniacs who
claim that cancer research can be performed *without*
animals. I've heard their bull shit about computers being the answer. They're trying to phase Doctor Rat out
with automation! The scoundrels! How can a compu-
terized answer ever replace the sight of a rat whose
lips are undergoing spontaneous amputation? How can
a mere machine and a little bit of human tissue culture
ever take the place of a living rat swelling with cancerous growths?

The half-assed Humaniacs say no animal ever
had or ever could have human cancer. I say, fuck off,
there are animals going to waste right now!

Look at them—all over the world, clumping
along, going to the meeting. Millions of basic models,
just waiting to be used. We mustn't let this experimental
material go to waste.

But how can we handle all this moving wildlife?
There just aren't enough trained dissectors available
to cut these bodies up and compare data. Even if we
stopped gassing beagles and boiling rabbits we couldn't
free enough good men to unravel all that flesh. I mean,
the proper dissection of a single rat takes three quarters
of an hour. Think how long it would take to hack open
that fucking giraffe!

Of course, there are millions of high-school students all over the world who are just getting their first
lessons in dissection. They've learned some of the tissue
paths of the living frog. Yes, and they've taken apart
the scrotal sac of a rat, they've gotten that sound foun-
dation under them. Why not enlist them to help control this uprising? We've already taught them how to

view rats, guinea pigs, and frogs. They know the truth, that these creatures are here to serve mankind's curiosity. Let's go, boys and girls! Follow Doctor Rat! Lift your scalpels high and immerse the skinned carcass in water! Watch the flesh rot away! Dissect the head from the spinal column, hurray! Save your old toothbrushes to scrub the flesh off the bones of your basic models! And mount the skeletons for all to see! You're on the way to Liberty! (I believe I've got another hit song coming out of all this, but I don't have time to brush up the lyrics now.) Onward, Dissecting Soldiers!

Doctor Rat's Youth Program. It can't fail. Train them from the cradle. Give your child a disintegrating mouse in a bottle and watch that child's eyes light up with interest as the flesh falls away, day by day.

Great sulphurated potash, what an idea!

Come along, children, and let's bore a hole through the orbital cavity! Oh hi-diddle-diddle, the cat on the griddle, having a heatstroke at noon. The little dog died under very hot lights, and we scooped out his eyes with a spoon!

Now, children, put on your rubber gloves and let's boil some bones.

This is my finest hour. It's clear to me now—I must start Children's Dissecting Clubs all over the globe. We'll meet every Tuesday after school and with Mom's help we'll skin a rodent. By the time Dad comes home, we'll have the water boiling gently and he can watch us dunk the body in.

Won't that be fun, boys and girls! You'll all receive a rat's skull-and-crossbones insignia for your jacket. And a skull pin for your beanie.

All the children marching, round and round the room. And every single Tuesday, we dissect someone's womb.

I've got to implement this program at once: letters to the various superintendents of schools, and to the Congress. I'll have to dip into my obscure statistics file and frame the proper ambiguous request for funds. A simple enough matter: ecology, sociology, relation-

ships, comparison, in light of recent studies, formation, orientation, blah, blah, blah. I've done it many
times before.

But time, Rat, time is the problem. The animals
are already marching.

My great humanistic dream must be temporarily
postponed. But we devoted researchers know how to
wait. Enlisting the children in this program is a definite direction-finding breakthrough. I'm surprised my
learned colleagues haven't enlarged upon it before.
True, they've produced the proper stimulus-response
formation in the minds of high-school students, but
what fertile ground we have in grammar-school kids!
They're naturally curious; they know all about pulling
the wings off a fly. We simply upgrade their natural
tendency and show them how to cut the nuts off a dog.

This is the sort of program that can catapult me
into a high government post. I've got to play my cards
right. But I know the kids will respond to dissection.
Oh, we can have such fun together. We'll get a chimpanzee and we'll cut off his head. Good. Then we'll
stuff the head. And then we'll bring another chimpanzee into the classroom and show him the stuffed head.
It will scare the shit out of him. Why? I am indebted
to Professor Austin for his explanation of this phenomenon, which he demonstrated very often to his own
students. The chimp is scared shitless of the stuffed
head because it has only a *few* of the ordinary char-
acteristics of a chimpanzee—i.e., eyes, nose, mouth,
and ears.

Live chimp looks at stuffed head. Shits pants.
Now, students, please observe what Professor Austin
has so skillfully pointed out: The scared chimp is suffering from *neophobia*. He's never before seen a head
just like his own resting on top of a desk. It's a new
experience—and so he runs like hell around the classroom, screaming.

He isn't screaming because he thinks they'll cut
off his head next. No, no, no, students, gracious no.
Nothing so morbid as that. It's just a little case of
neophobia.

It's important for young students to make such

subtle distinctions, and I can help them to do so, in a fun way. (A grammar-school program must have fun instruction like this headless chimpy game.)

I'll be leading the entire field with this thing; the doors of the White House are going to open to Doctor Rat. A scientist occasionally spies his destiny and I see mine. It's with the children. This is a profound moment in history, and I, who am trained in perceiving the delicate unreleasing stimuli, am getting a terrific rush out of this one. Doctor Rat will be dining with the President of the United States!

I'll have grants coming out of my ears.

In the meantime, while this valuable scientific idea is incubating in my cerebral hemispheres, I've got to set up a counterrevolutionary receiving set and find out what man is doing to squash this revolution. Over here, beyond the pickled fetuses is a small abandoned activity drum which will do fine. The smaller sets give you sharper pictures, anyway.

All right, I'm climbing through the door and putting my paws on the wire floor. Now run, Doctor, run!

Get this goddamn thing spinning fast enough . . . I'm in as good shape as ever . . . my experimental psychosis has lent a certain vigor to all my motor systems. I can show a clean heel when I have to, gentlemen. The Albino Flash! Wow, this wheel is really singing . . . should facilitate some good reception . . . now to jump off and watch the picture coming in. . . .

Okay, I've got a perfect seat, and here comes the highly classified counterrevolutionary signal. Good, excellent, a special meeting of the military advisors. This is the kind of show I love! Nothing namby-pamby in it. Straight fast decision-making on the highest level. These are your best men in an emergency. You don't want any ecological conservatives around at times like this. They're all right in their place, mind you, beautifying the roadsides, but in the short-term view, when you need action in a hurry for results *now,* those boys aren't the ones to call.

And I'm happy to see the African leaders realize this.

"Mr. President, as you know, the Research Programme for Gathering a Selective Cross-section of the Species has been formed rather quickly. But the animals have already collected in such vast numbers that we couldn't afford to hesitate."

"I'm aware of the need for immediate action, Mr. Secretary."

"Yes, sir. We have some very good men in the Programme and they've flown over the areas where the animals are gathered. The numbers have been assessed and the conclusion is that the proposed cross-section can be taken without significant damage to any of the species."

"You've conferred with the Minister of Natural Resources?"

"The Minister is of the opinion that a considerable harvesting of the elephant and hippo groups is essential. His teams have observed that these particular groups have become too successful and are in need of cropping-out. In the long run, the herds will benefit by such selective harvesting. We are, in fact, hoping to achieve a lasting dynamic balance of the animal population. This massing of the animals makes the implementation of that part of the Programme much easier. A better ecology, sir, is going to be the end result."

"I'm happy to hear that, Mr. Secretary. In your memorandum you mentioned certain economic benefits . . ."

"The Research Programme will pay for itself, sir, many times over."

"Exactly how will that work, Mr. Secretary?"

"Sir, as soon as we realized that the herds were gathering in such great numbers we invited tenders from the larger American and European pet food companies. Those tenders have now been received."

"May I see them, Mr. Secretary?"

"Yes, sir, here they are. As you can see—"

"The figures are substantial."

"Very substantial, Mr. President."

"And how is the Selective Cross-section going to be gathered?"

"I've already conferred with Air Marshal Mobogo. He's very enthusiastic about a Selective Harvest of this size as it will give his air force a lifelike military maneuver in which to test out our new Phantom jets."

"Have you spoken to Shudite?"

"General Shudite is eager to test his own new machinery under battlefield conditions. The gathered elephants, for example, are quite similar in size to a tank battalion. The general is certain that valuable field maneuvers will result."

We sit and groom each other, picking out fleas and watching the many animals as they enter the plain. The noise is tremendous, and yet a gentle calm seems to pervade the ranks. We gorillas who have always lived in solitude upon the jungle heights can only sit in wonder here, in the midst of so much activity.

The leopard blinks at me sleepily and licks his paws. No one moves to attack us. The great black buffalo is chewing the grass. A little rhinoceros has come in amongst the elephants, playfully nudging them with her horn. And the leopard cubs are playing with the hyenas!

I feel I should stand up and pound my chest. But there is no need to do so. The air is filled with contentment and a wonderful expectation. I scratch my head.

The exercise wheel is slowing down, the picture is getting weaker. I've got to get back on the wheel again and generate some more intuitive kilopower.

Enemy patrol coming this way! Quick, Rat, go into disguise. . . .

Taking my tail in my mouth, I start to chase it, round and round, exhibiting all the activity of a rat caught in a compulsive syndrome. There are many such rats in the lab, all of whom were driven into this tail-chasing psychosis by the Learned Professor. I look just like one of them, going faster and faster.

The enemy patrol is slowing down, coming closer.

"Hello, in there! Can we help you?"

I spin madly on, eyes closed, whirling round and round.

"He's too far gone . . . a hopeless case. . . ."

A masterful subterfuge. The rebels are marching away. And this spinning round and round is producing a very strong intuitive field. Yes, here comes a strong signal now, straight from Washington. Hurrah, boys! Let's deal with these revolutionaries in the one sure way of effecting a just and lasting peace!

"The Wildlife Department says they have no way of tranquilizing so many animals. By the time they get all the animals knocked out here, at Point B, those they knocked out earlier at Point A will be waking up, before a single animal's been moved. And there are such great numbers of the smaller animals that the rangers can't even make a dent."

"Can't they make a hell of a lot of noise or something and scare them all back into the woods? High-frequency whistles, maybe, to drive the animals away?"

"Every state is claiming that *herds* of deer are involved, as well as large groups of other big animals, like bears. If you tried to move them that way, you'd have them spilling out all over the highways. There'd be a traffic pile-up like nobody's seen before. It'd cripple the nation."

"Some environmental honcho is claiming it's been caused by DDT in the food chain."

". . . behaviorists talking about the psychosis of mass exodus . . ."

"Gentlemen, the President is not interested at the moment in why it's happened. He wants an action memo with his options for bringing about a solution, fast."

"We can't possibly coordinate the wildlife agencies of every little town in the country. They're panicked anyway. I've talked to enough idiots today to know we've got no chance of solving this on the local level."

"Have we talked to the Pentagon yet? The army's probably got some kind of gas that will tranquilize whole herds. . . ."

The enemy patrols have all passed by, Rat. Now is your great moment. Quietly as a tiny Eurasian Harvest Mouse I creep along, intent on reaping a full harvest of revolutionary heads. (Dissection of trachea and main vessels. I might also deliver a few kidneys. And pass a sharp needle through the thyroid gland. And transplant their adrenal glands to their groin. Ha ha!)

But first I must fashion a gas mask, if I'm going to make a successful raid on the Chemical Closet. Here, among the cleaning tools, I nibble away a piece of sponge large enough to cover my whole head. Quickly, Rat, hollow it out, make eye holes and ear holes. Nose and mouth must remain covered. It's a crude device, but I haven't time to write a requisition in triplicate for a proper gas mask.

Now, down this last aisle, quickly. Scurry, scurry, duck.

Hidden in the shadow of the table leg, I look all around, right and left. Go, Doctor, go!

"No, you don't!"

A Growth Hormone goon leaps in front of me. The bastard's bigger than a Gambian Pouched Rat. But I arch my back and begin tooth-chattering (cf. "Rat Rage," Broome and Poole, *Psy. Post,* 1967).

His back raises up, his hair is bristling. He snaps at me, misses, and I sink my teeth into his tail. "Back, you mangy overgrown mouse! Cf. *Territorial Defense,* Sloan and Wilson, 1960."

He bites again, but I charge him head down and drive into his gut, bowling him over. Doctor Rat is

177

light, fast, and blessed with hysterical energy, my friend. You don't take him without a fight!

A scalpel lying here on the floor. I pick it up quickly and wave it wildly, chasing off the goon.

But other swordsmen are gathering, armed with picks, chisels, drill bits. "Disperse at once, you rabble!"

I have no fear of them, I, a Learned Mad Doctor with high scores in Competitive Behavior. "Come on, fellow rats. I shall be happy to initiate you into the mysteries of my slogan. Death . . . is freedom!"

Fighting them off, clanging here, beating there, I move backward up the clothes tree, fighting on the edge of this carved-claw foot. Very well, if I must die here I shall, but I'll take some of these bastards with me . . . beat . . . parry . . . thrust. . . .

Sweet Suffering Pack Rats! (genus *Neotoma*) Advancing upon me are the ring-collared females. Oh, they're a hideously vicious bunch. By fastening a ring to their necks we were able to keep them from washing themselves, thus producing an experimental psychosis. When they had their babies, they refused to wash them and, instead, ate them.

And now they're trying to eat me! Son of a titmouse!

"Back . . . back, you bitches!"

Too many of them. But I refuse to die such an ignominious death as being eaten alive by these lunatics. I turn, leaping up the clothes tree, clambering toward the white uniform hanging there.

Quick, into the pocket!

Down here in the dark—only a temporary respite. They're rocking the clothes tree. They'll knock it over. What is this envelope in here, a government grant, perhaps?

Hmmmmm, it's filled with a strange white powder. I'll just have a look at this paper and see what it says. . . .

Cocaine! Pure-grade government research lab cocaine! I've never had it before, but I'm familiar with the literature and I know what to do!

Snort snort

Snort snort

BONG BONG BONG BONG BONG BONG BONG BONG BONG BONG BONG BONG

Let me at them! I'll tear them to pieces, where are they—I'm crawling out of this pocket and leaping . . .

DOCTOR SUPER RAT!

Landing in the midst of the enemy, knocking them right and left. Wheels going off in my brain. Doctor Rat is on!

Power, raw burning Peruvian power. Racing toward the Chemical Closet I make my bid. The rebel guard is changing, saluting with their tails, *Social Behavior,* etc., and I rush them.

Snarling, biting, kicking, there, take that, you . . . years of frustration . . . punishment . . . stimulus . . .

"Stop him, bring him down!"

"You sniveling rat's asshole, I'll . . ." Incentive for correct response, socking, nipping . . . modification kick in the balls . . . Turner and Murdock . . . enlarged adrenals . . . knocking the bastards aside, fighting my way into the depth of the Closet.

"Call for reinforcements! It's Doctor Rat!"

Motivating factors, punch in the eyeball . . . reward . . . Blumfield and Coltz diffusion panels crash . . . nobody fucks with Doctor Rat . . . bite off your tail . . . midsagittal section of the upper incisor . . . berserker rage . . . multiple lefts and rights, fast combinations, bowling them over. . . . Christ, here come the hooded rats, and those boys are really frustrated, *Five Hooded Rats in the Discrimination Box,* Drake and Akins.

Bite him in the guts . . . gotcha, you hooded freak . . . interspecific conflict, seizing and biting, cf., watch out, over there, leaping and biting intervals, *Boxing Rats,* Geoffrey and Doyle . . . getting close to the chemical shelves . . . if I can only . . . mixing aggression with attempts at coitus, that really spooks them, fucked by a Mad Doctor, come on you sons-of-bitches, Doctor Rat's got something for you . . . hair raised, urinating and defecating, the works, moving round them, back maximally arched, holding them off as I edge to the shelf.

"Get him! Don't let him up there!"

Rapidly striking with the forelimbs, scratching with the back paws, pain-causing stimulus evoking flight amongst my enemies, now!

I've made it to the first shelf. Quickly, then, to the top, to the top secret chemical warfare bottles. Thanks to all this superb research, seventy-six enemy children died in Rattankirir Province near the Vietnamese border. Ha ha! Twisting my tail around the di-nitrophenol, I let it fly!

Die, you goddamn gooks! Die in the name of Claude Bernard and Uncle Sam!

"Man is coming! Look, banana mice, man is coming through the trees!"

How suddenly he has appeared. Why does he wear the bushes of the jungle on his head? Now he approaches us, like a tree that walks.

But the meeting is complete! We'll surge together with man. We'll know the wonderful moments of all hearts beating as one!

Look overhead! Man has sent his great lifeless birds to greet us! How loud they are! How they roar, these lifeless birds. But don't run, animals. Be steady. Now our meeting can truly begin.

The gorillas walk forward with hands raised over their heads in the gesture of receiving.

The dinitrophenol explodes magnificently on the floor, its spirit ascending into the air, the spirit of our laboratory, defending me. How wrathful she looks in her yellow gown, with her long vicious teeth shining. Wildly she sweeps over the rebels and they fall, covered with burns, blinded, vomiting. What a terrible smell, worse than a starved monkey's fart.

Over go some more bottle bombs—dinitricorte, acid disclophenocyncetic, arsenic anhydride, calcium cyanide. Every pregnant rat in the laboratory miscarries immediately. Fewer rebels to swell the ranks! I've got you now, you chinky bitches! (cf. *The Women of Lam Dong Province,* Medical Diary of Dr. Nguyen, Russell War Crimes Tribunal)

I'm defoliating their ranks now, thinning them out with a few more bombs, chlorophenyl-dimethylurea and dichlorophenyl-dimethylurea, go, boys, go! Down they sail, end over end, and burst open. Sending out the death cloud (cf. *The 18,000 Inhabitants of Da Nang, Natus Disease, 1,000 Dead,* Japanese Science Council Report, 1967). Terrific! This is real power now! Doctor Rat has saved the day!

I wonder what special tranquilizing gas the army is using in *its* huge maneuver?

"This is Able Baker One to Red Fox Two. Do you read me, Red Fox Two?"

"Go ahead, Able Baker."

"This is General Denver. I want machine guns sweeping that far ridge. . . ."

Run, cub, run!

"Momma . . . Momma . . ."

She's fallen, she cannot run. The ground all around us is exploding. The terrible insects of man are whizzing through the air. Get up, cub, get up!

". . . help me . . . help, Momma . . ."

The insects have bitten her. Blood flows from her side. I shall carry you, little cub, in my teeth. You aren't heavy.

Many have fallen. The deer, the moose, the foxes —all dead, stung by the loud flaming insects of death. I've got you in my teeth, little one. How light you are . . .

The crying, such crying, as a great moose charges toward the men, his horns lowered. I must reach the trees. What is the sting of a bee—nothing, nothing compared to this. The ground is writhing with stung rabbits and raccoons. The bobcats are crawling, screeching. Such confusion, rolling clouds, which way . . . I've lost the forest! The cloud parts, a giant shadow steps before me.

"This way . . ."

Through the cloud I plunge, to follow him. So we meet again. Where are the spring flowers? Men everywhere, with their stinging lights, the deadly bees who bite deeply. A proud stag falls, tumbling through the ashes of this dump, and we leap over his twistng legs.

I follow the large dark shape of my husband, and we run, fear and death screaming beside us. The great shadow of my mate turns to me.

"Your cub is dead. Release her."

184

How heavily her head hangs. Her eyes stare into mine, but she has left them.

"Come!" He sinks his teeth into my shoulder, tearing me free from the cub.

Running together, our bodies touch, as when we ran through the meadow. The porcupines are squealing, rolling in the ashes, their bellies ripped open. We run through them; why did we come here? I can't remember now. It's all gone. The terrible stinging has pierced our reason; we are maddened and bleeding. Quick, husband, I'm beside you. We'll find the forest and go deep, never venturing here again.

Flames ahead! We whirl, leaping this way . . .

He roars, rising on his back legs, spinning in a tall overwhelming dance. Red words burst from his tongue and I too have been stung. But run with me, run!

Our paws meet in the air. His eyes gaze into mine. We are upon the spring meadow, my love, dancing in the warm light. Do you hear the swallows singing sweetly and can you smell the honeycomb?

". . . Ed Hanson for CBS here in the stockyard. The entire area is marked off into combat zones, and the dogs and steers are being driven toward blind alleys and walls. Police are being assisted by armored cars. An armored car to the left there . . . you can see it nosing out of the alleyway. Six stampeding steers trying for the main street! The gunfire from the armored car reaches them, and the steers are down! There are dogs on every side of us, snarling, attacking everything in sight. The street is running with blood . . . I think we can make a switch now . . . can we switch over to John Cooke . . . John, take it from there . . ."

". . . in what police have designated as the southeast quadrant of their massive encircling maneuver. I'm with Captain Arthur Briscomb, who's in charge of the operation. Captain, what's the situation right now?"

"We're evacuating all the buildings in this area. Some of the steers are inside. They broke through doors and windows. There's heavy gunfire, with the use of gas rifles. We want all citizens to stay clear of this area and to avoid contact with any dogs."

"Has the force suffered casualties, Captain?"

"We've got ambulances and medical people all around here."

"The number of dead animals . . ."

"The job isn't a pretty one."

"Thank you, Captain. This is John Cooke for . . ."

186

Doctor Rat wins! Yes, Humaniacs, take a little bit of this! Down go the special Army Mixtures, Agent Blue, Agent Orange, and Agent White. Down, down, down, the secret chemical agents float, exploding open. Ha ha, look at the rebels backing away from the rainbow of death! They can't escape. What horrible shapes I've released, one after another, morbid and foaming, fists of steel knocking the rebels over. Agent Blue is spreading everywhere with his secret commando corps, their fangs dripping, claws sharp and shining. I'll get the Distinguished Service Medal for this day's work! Memo to the Defense Supply Agency:

Gentlemen:
Thanks to our suppliers—Dow, Diamond Alkali, Uniroyal, Thompson Chemical, Monsanto, Ansul, and Thompson Hayward—I have managed to contribute my share to our lasting peace.

Dead rebels everywhere, males, females, ratlings. Look at them crawling and gagging. There's no escape, you Commies! Your colony has been wiped out, and your cages contaminated for years to come. This is what you get for your rebellious activity, for sympathizing with those dirty dogs on the treadmill. Aiding and abetting the enemy. Well, take this!

Down go the bottle bombs, how wonderful they look when they burst open and spread. God is on our side, and this is the proof of it. Those pantywaists at Harvard and MIT who protested chemical agents should see what happens when you let a revolution get

187

ahead of you. This is big business, gentlemen; we're talking about five hundred million dollars' worth of contracts. I regret a few noncombatants got smoked out. So we killed a few rabbits and some cats. What can I tell you? All these gooks are alike, if you ask me.

"From the Halls of Mus Musculus
to the shores of Y-Maze-D . . ."

Singing and fighting I carry on. Upon the battlements I stride, one rat alone. Fighting for international good-will and a better world, I dump enough defoliants to burn the hair off a brass monkey's balls, taking care to select those areas in which most harm will be done to the guerrillas and least harm to local populations, covering everything in sight.

My shell has been crushed. A giant rumbling thing passed over me and I lie broken in the dust. Now the riddle is in pieces, the lines of fate and fortune marred, distorted, and the meaning of my life a-jumble. I am a shellful of blood.

The sound of men's voices fill the air. They rolled over me.

I crawl feebly, a ruined oracle in the animal's graveyard. There is no future for us. My broken lines indicate extinction; I saw it as I split in two. I feel the shattered network of our kingdom. The mutilated lions moan their secret names, crying out that which they've long held secret. Now my legs refuse to move. My blood trickles from the living cup, and stains the sand.

Man came to the meeting. He attended in great numbers.

I must find shade, but it's impossible to withdraw into my shell. The dome is wrecked and does not admit me any longer. What a fine home it was; what peaceful dreams and meditations I had inside there, securely enclosed, protected. The finest of homes is eventually undone.

Men's voices nearing, and their shadow falls upon my cracked carapace. I'm lifted, tossed into a dark sack. The sack swings back and forth. The shade I wanted is mine, but with it is blended the design of man.

The sack swings back and forth, back and forth. In the distance the monkeys scream their curses; but man answers with his more powerful curse, the ear-piercing whine and clatter. And the monkeys are silent.

The lowing of the hippos takes up the dying chant —the deep *ba - ho - ho - ho* which we have heard on peaceful nights. We hear it now, in the burning day, and man replies, and we hear it no more. Man's voice silences all.

The sack is opened, I am falling to the ground. I can't withdraw into the shell. Men's laughing voices. There is the sound of fire. They hold me now.

Pounding me with stones. Sharp through the roof. Cracking completely open. My body is naked. They tear me from my shell. They hold me up, laughing at my puny nakedness. I don't care, for my only interest is to turn, to squirm, to see the shell at last, to see its outer surface.

They toss me through the air, through steam— burning water! Naked, boiling, I flounder . . . salt fire . . . trying to rise . . . the cup . . . I drink the fire. . . .

". . . John Cooke for CBS News here in Chicago, at the outskirts of the city, where the sanitation department has started bringing the carcasses from another day of slaughter. A huge incinerator is spewing forth the smoke from thousands of burning bodies. The sky has been darkened by the smoke . . . a truck coming now . . . the carcasses are all mangled and crushed . . . giant claws and shovels scoop out piles of bullet-riddled dogs and cattle.

"Flesh and bones, oozing tangles of intestines, with horned heads and matted tails strung on them. Hoofs and stiffened legs are sticking out between the great iron teeth of the machinery. The huge fork moves —the head of a dead beagle is speared right on the end of one of the fork's tines.

"And the incinerator continues to belch forth flames as the bodies are dumped into it, here in the city where the animal uprising may have had its first beginnings. Now the mass exodus, as it is being called by the biologists, has spread everywhere. Scenes like this are being enacted around the globe, as the hysterically surging animal nation undergoes its most terrible hour.

"John Cooke, CBS News, Chicago . . ."

Yikes! The rebels are regrouping and advancing again. Look at them coming, with their dogs and monkeys. They're approaching stealthfully, and I must stand here alone, defending the nation! Very well, if I must I will. Doctor Rat is no pantywaist. He'll fight the guerrilla forces with everything at his disposal. Telegram to Edgewood Arsenal, Dover, New Jersey: *Keep it coming, Fellow Patriots!*

I see that still stronger measures are called for. So over to the most devastating collection of bottles known to man, over here, at the far end of the shelf, to Defense Department Contract AD-13-045-AML-164. We're getting 350 million bucks a year for this one, friends, us and fifty other American universities—see *Viet Report,* 1969. It's high-class stuff, the cream of the crop, good old bubonic plague!

Go, bub, go!

Down he goes, crashing open on the floor, a masterfully developed strain resistant to all antibiotics! We've been working on it for years. Look at it spreading. Hurray, hurray! (cf., twenty-two out of twenty-nine provinces north of Saigon hit by plague).

Oh, this is great stuff. Those bacilli are tough little bastards. The Learned Professor and I have been developing them now—go, go—for ten years, highly pathogenic.

Thanks to the cooperation of Cornell, we've determined the most effective way to deliver these agents (see *Science Mag.,* Feb. 23, 1967).

"Gimme a *B,* gimme a *U,* gimme a *B,* gimme an

O, gimme an *N*, gimme an *I*, gimme a *C! Bubonic, bubonic, bubonic*, go!" Look at him charging through that line, Cornell defenders all around him, trampling over the rebels. Touchdown!

My old tusks are lowered, the mighty shivering instinct is upon me. I feel young again. I shiver among the other bulls. We make a mighty charge. Forward, bulls, we must charge through them to the jungle. I know a river we can all go to.

Beware men's tusks of fire. His tusks speak fire and thunder. Our leader moves us forward and we turn as he turns. Largest animal on the plain, great bull, lead us to the jungle. As in the old days, the grand days of my youth, I am beside you again.

We see and smell the distant forest and we'll eat there tonight. We'll stand beneath the trees at twilight and munch down the green leaves. Don't stand in the way of our dinner, little pygmy, or we'll shatter you down. We are the mustering!

Can you thunder this loud! Can you shake the plains, pygmy, like this! We shake the plains and you are as puny as a gnat. You're all the same to us, little beasts of prey, and we shall trample you down!

Herd leader menacing forward, his ears out wide, as we approach them in the enormity of our front view, our ears spread out wide. We are the biggest elephants in the world.

Rise up thunder shaking. Run over the sands. We are the forward-charging elephant with ears out, breaking through man's tusks of fire.

Tumbling . . . the herd thundering past me. I crawl on the sands as they thunder past me. Something has struck me in the belly. Too old for the mustering . . . too old . . .

". . . here at our special CBS Control Center for the Animal Crisis. The latest reports continue to confirm the global proportions of the crisis. In what biologists now call an unprecedented radiation of the instinctive urge toward mass movement, the animals have gathered in tremendous groups on every continent. Many of these gathering places are remote, but others are quite close to major cities. In Kinshasa, Jim Winthrop reports:"

"From the top of Stanley Hill, one can see Kinshasa spread out below—wharves, skyscrapers, building cranes—a modern city on the move. And in the streets, herds of antelope frantically stampeding. On the steps of the Roman Catholic cathedral, a dead water buffalo, his huge head wedged against the door. In the big central square, the Armée Nationale has its hands full with charging wild boars and menacing cats. On every street one sees abandoned automobiles, and the normally overflowing sidewalk cafés are deserted—except for the animals who wander aimlessly and fearfully through the overturned tables and chairs.

"Along the banks of the Congo, the coffee, palm, and rubber plantations have suffered severe damage from the great stampeding herds and from the army troops and heavy equipment which is in pursuit of them.

"In every direction, on all the highways and byroads, the animals have appeared, caught in the movement, driven by unnamable instinctual forces which have thrown the Congo into yet another war, this one the strangest and most terrible, by far, that it has ever fought. Jim Winthrop, CBS News, Kinshasa . . ."

I lie on the great plain with death inside me, with death sunk deep into me. My trunk is all that is left to me; I stretch it out, but it fills with dust. I have toppled. My tusks are dug into the sand. I thought to die by the river, but it was not to be.

I hear the screaming of the she-lions; upon the wind is the sighing of the hippo. He opens his mouth to the sky, to swallow it, to live a moment longer. From the corner of my eye I see him on his back, his stumpy legs in the air. He was too fat to fare well on this plain. But he wanted to come. They all wanted to be here. It was worth having been here, in the one moment when we surged. Then I felt us all united. Then I saw the meaning of the earth. Could I have forgotten it already?

Yes, I've forgotten. I'm old and badly wounded. And were I to speak the little bit I remember of the surging moment, the fierce badger would bite me.

The smoke is drifting over us. We lie in a heap, the quivering elephant nation. The mightiest bulls are fallen beside me, their tongues hanging out, their eyes staring into the sand. We bought the one moment with our blood. It seems a high price to pay, but we stood imperturbable, in the knowledge.

I don't feel any sharp teeth. The badgers are all dead. But even so, I cannot elaborate further on the surging. We touched our trunks, we were one. I miss the riverbank. It isn't easy to die. All my careful preparations—it isn't easy. My breath is leaving me. My breath is departing. I'm sorry for the young ones, for the newborn calves. They barely tasted the sweet leaves.

My breath goes further . . . I cannot call it back. The path is black. This is the great fear. The plums, the plums . . .

They'll make shoes out of me if they catch me. They'll be wearing this old chimp on their feet. I went to the center of the plain, like the old fool I am. Went and got trapped.

Desire to test the Great One Animal led us here. Desire to be the One Great Animal, to feel the power of his kingdom.

Feel it trembling now, feel it trembling about us, the thunder of war. They love it; we are their sport. Terrified trembling nation, thunder on the plains, my body keeping the awesome drumbeat. Their drums are much louder than ours. What chimp can drum as loud as you, oh man! We cannot match your mighty *tr-ump tr-ump!* Our tree-stump drums are too small. We couldn't sound like you.

This way, rush through the yellow sand, over the fallen bodies of the others. Must make the jungle wall. Must reach the treetops again.

We wanted to know the One Animal, and man had to be there too. For one moment of completeness we give our life. We bought it with our life, but we had it, masters. We had our illumination. We all stood together on the plain with you. We appreciated our perfect plain with you.

We had the one moment.

Down, bend your head low, chimp. Crawl along through the hairy bodies. Fur all around me, much trembling, blood-oozing. Man, the animal, with his fiery horns.

Man's horns of fire.

Playing his drum of mightiness.

Roar, roar!

This old chimp is going to make the jungle wall. They haven't seen me yet. I'll get away. Get back to the little babbling stream and dream beside it all day long. Never go away from it, never leave it. Listen to it night and day. I want to listen to you, little stream, lead me back to you. You are magic, this I know. Help the old chimp now, give him your protection, guide him by your magic power.

Baby chimp on the sand. Pick him up, scoop him in my arms. "Hang on to me. Wrap your arms around my neck." Now which way do I go? Man's horns of fire everywhere. His magic is great.

Baby chimp's heart pounds against my back. He cries. I run. Babbling little stream, help us get to you. Help us through the horns of fire. If I can get to you and plunge into you, little stream, we'll be saved. Nobody will be near us, for you are far back in the forest where man has never been.

Talk to the little babbling stream as we run, child. Pray to it for guidance. Seek its spirit with your call. It is our only hope, for we're on the open plain.

A fog of smoke, shadows moving through it. The gorilla spins, struck by a flaming stone. How does man hurl the stones so fast?

Must reach the green wall, dive into the jungle. Drink from the flower cups. Pour the flower water on my head. Splash in the little stream. Blue flowers filled with cool water. Guide me, little flowers, guide me through the fire. I've got the little chimp. We're trying to get to you. The great plain is vast, holding so many. Giants thundering all around us. But through the smoke, the jungle appears to me. Not far now, little chimp, hold on tight.

The last few steps—into the green! Grab the vine and go. Go, old chimp, faster than you ever went before. Don't let the little one fall. We made the jungle, little chimp, the stream is guiding us. The power of the stream will guide us on.

With the soft green all around us. Covered in grass now nobody sees us. Saved by the green. Always the green. Follow it to safety. The open plain is not for us. We are the denizens of the treetops. Swinging through the treetops. This old chimp can climb. I'll take you far away, child. This stream I'm thinking of, this stream we're praying to, is filled with bright faces. You'll see your ears sticking out there. Hold tight to me, for I'll move without stopping.

What more could we ask from life, little stream, but the sight of you rippling and playing in the light? You are wiser than a thousand elephants. You pour wisdom over our heads, and you lead me.

"Sergeant, what's moving in that treetop?"
  "Very good, Captain, I shall attend to it at once."

I lower my horn. Man's great lifeless rhinos grind toward me, their long straight horns snorting fire. They snort once and the lions are ripped apart. We must learn to make fire come out of our horns.

The chimps are all dead, and the great gorilla leaders have pounded their chests in vain. The lifeless beasts of men roll over them. Even the elephants are losing, every charge they make ending in a quivering fall. But these snorting clanking beasts of man will not find me so easy to kill. They won't kill a rhino so easily. I'll plunge my horn through the heart of man's monster.

My wrath should never be provoked. My wrath is a terrible thing. You'll feel my wrath, monster.

But many dying beasts block my path. Open for me, animals! I want to use my horn!

I go forward, pushing through the dying herds. Our great meeting has been ruined. For a moment we lifted our heads and became one animal. Now I pad along blindly through the dust. I am an old beast, and I've heard the lion strike at dawn, but never have I known such dying as today.

Snorting monster, I hear you. I hear the cries of the animals struck down. I'm searching you out with my horn.

"Don't step on Great Silence, mighty rhino."

"No, ostrich, I'm short-sighted but him I see. I wouldn't step upon his body."

I see the monster before me. I see him moving there, where he snorts at the lioness, blowing her into the air with his flaming trunk. He's mine now, I'll take him down.

Thunder, great rhino. This is the time. Bring it all forward into your shoulders and horn. Bring your many days forward now, bring it all forward, the fields and the trees and the skies you have seen. Bring it all into this rush.

I think I'd better throw in some typhoid too. Here, my dear, the good Doctor Rat is going to let you out for an airing. What a pretty cloud, floating over the lab. Rebels dropping in their tracks as they breathe it. Yes, she's a mean lady, multiplying rapidly, right through the colony, knockin' 'em dead!

They haven't got a chance. I might as well mix in some dysentery, with a little glanders, and some anthrax, shoving them off the shelf. The good Doctor mixing up a brew for you, here in the secret storehouse. It's coming, it's coming at you. Ah, they float down, *crash* they break open, *woosh* they float off.

Bacilli, wild and shivering with rage. The spirits in this Chemical Closet are amazing. I love them so. Pilot to bombardier: Bombs away!

Down goes the special container of spiders carrying good old hemorrhagic anthrax meningitis. Furry crawling black spiders, leaving the bottle bomb, and moving toward the enemy (cf. *The K'uan-Tien Incident*, March 12, 1952, International Scientific Commission Report).

Pilot to bombardier: Let's give them one more. There's a bottle of fleas here carrying a dynamite strain of *pasteurella pestis*. It'd be a shame not to use it. Down through the dark night it goes, caught in the rebel searchlight. But they can't stop it. Biological warfare can't be beaten. The bottle explodes, scattering the fleas. Off they hop, looking for their victims.

Here come the Growth Hormone Rats after me!

They're carrying the Aeroil Torch! The bastards are setting fire to the Chemical Closet!

Flames leaping into the air. I hurl a cholera capsule at them, exploding it at their feet, but the damage has been done. The shelves are crackling and swaying, smoke rising all around me.

I scurry down the braces. Oh, this is horrible, everything burning, the lab ravaged by fire. Enemy troops are closing in, moving through the curling smoke, but I slip into the gray curtain, hiding in the swirling clouds.

"There he is. Take him!"

Hooded rats advance toward me. If only I can get to pen and paper and make my last official statement in the Newsletter. History will read it and history will be my judge. I must get to the desk over . . .

. . . the floor collapses and I find myself beneath the laboratory, in amongst the beams. This, then, is my final bunker. I sought to lead my people to their destiny, on the surgical table, and they have betrayed me. My empire has been destroyed. My paws are shaking.

Horrible. Allied shadows move overhead—the dogs, the frogs.

Your unicorn has attended the feast. My white flesh intrigues you, and my spiraling horn. I dance here among the fallen, but you can't see me, no. I came from the plain of the highlands, beyond what you can know. But you attended, you made me attend. We had the one meeting, whose purpose you shall never know. You served a purpose, you came today. The One Animal needed you, prepared you, and sought you out today. You will never know the reason why. The One Animal is beyond all of us. I am but a veil across his dream. This hour is but a turning in his sleep. And yet . . ."

We needed you, man, for the One Animal's dream.

". . . as president of the Toshido Fisheries, I'm honored by your presence at the stockholders' meeting. Ten thousand echoes of good fortune resound throughout the entire whaling industry. The unseasonal and unprecedented migration of such vast whale herds into the offshore waters has saved us millions in manpower, storage, and shipping of the product. . . ."

I crawled to the mountaintop to see the eagles and I slithered back down to attend the great meeting.

I've been caught and nailed to a tree.

The nail is through my neck. I hang, lashing my body. Men move from tree to tree, where other snakes hang. They took all the bright ones. On each tree hangs a brightly colored snake, with a nail through its neck.

We hang in the meadow. The eagles were killed by men's lifeless birds. Each time I move the nail tortures my nerves. We hang, decorating the trees.

The eagles' hearts no longer sound the drum. The drums are silenced. We hang in the heat of the day. Now they come with their sharp tools.

He slices through my neck, down my body. And walks on. I am agony split open. Now comes another; he inserts his fingers into my neck. He tears the skin from my body! I see my skin in his hand! I hang raw, exposed and tormented. I hang raw upon the tree. The others hang beside me, their skins ripped off—there—torn off—there, another. We thrash and beat our anguished flesh against the bark.

All the bright skins are gone.

The flies land upon our raw streaming bodies.

"... for CBS in England, Malcom Pendennings brings us this report:"

"... there you see the just developed footage of the capture of the legendary beast. Two soldiers, Lieutenant Patterson and Corporal Davis, carrying the beast between them on a pole, the fabulous unicorn, slain on the field of battle. Lieutenant Patterson is with us in our studio now. You are the one who fired the shot that brought the unicorn down?"

"Yes sir, two rounds, at a distance of 250 yards."

I, the hyena, crawl to my water dish. Our leader, the Imperial Eagle, is dead. We felt him die; we were with him on the heights; we plunged with him to the earth and we crashed there, in a heap.

My legs are weak; I crawl back to the corner of my cage like a spotted shadow. There is nothing left for me now. In his glass cage the gorilla sits, staring into nothingness, soiling himself. The elephant is sprawled in his straw, no longer hungry, no longer caring to rise.

The birds have ceased their chatter, have stopped squawking over twigs and nesting space. Even the insane pelican, who usually defends his rock with hideous shrieks, has tucked his head under his wing. The rock which gave him stability and a shred of sanity has been abandoned.

I know now that I'm dying; the whole prison is in the grip of death. We flop about feebly. Our soul is withdrawing into its deepest cave; it no longer cares to live.

A bird has fallen on the lawn; he was no captive bird, but a free creature. He has fallen, and he is not the first to fall from the open sky.

I smell the day, the wet leaves, the grass. Through the years my only pleasure was in these smells, and even in my feebleness I still enjoy them. Their secret character is indeed clearer to me now than ever before. Each smell is a dancer in the air, dancing round me, intoxicating me. I try to rise, my legs won't hold me.

"Surpassing Slothfulness, why have you stopped shuffling along? We're not yet at the meeting place."

"Quickly, young fellow, take hold of a branch!"

"But you said we weren't to stop until we reached the meeting!"

"The meeting is ended. Didn't you feel it just now surrender?"

"Surrender?"

"Hang on, young sloth, if you value your life."

The old pile of moss displays surprising speed as he ambles toward a tree and mounts up the trunk to the limbs, where he takes his grip and immediately becomes a part of the foliage.

The hanging green nest dissects itself, the upper portion turning slowly, deliberately, toward me. A dark hole appears among the twigs, the moss. "Don't stand there gaping, you idiot. Grab a branch!"

I go to the trunk of the tree and slowly climb it. Selecting a branch beside Surpassing Slothfulness, I go down it, hand over hand, and take my position.

"What is going on, Master Surpassing?"

"Hang still and you'll know soon enough."

"Please, Master, I'm not as sensitive to the hidden winds as you are. What is going on?"

The old bunch of moss doesn't reply. I have no choice but to hang beside him and wait. Out of the corner of my eye I can discern a tiny raindrop hidden in the hanging pile of moss. It is the eye of the master; the twigs gently rearrange themselves and the raindrop is gone, covered by a green curtain.

Well, I know how to enjoy a rest period. I close

my own eyes and prepare for the long slow glide into sleep. But a soft whisper interrupts me:

"Don't sleep, young sloth. Cling tightly and stay awake."

"I'm very tired, sir."

"It's approaching now. It comes like a whirlwind. You've got to greet it with your eyes open."

"What's coming?"

"The Soul of the Animals. A tremendous number of them died today, all over the earth. It has loosened the thread that ties us to our bodies."

A sudden sadness overtakes me. I feel it now, searching its way through the jungle. The bird stops in mid-song.

"It will try to take you, young sloth."

"I'm holding fast."

"Now . . . now it blows over us. . . ."

The whirlwind has touched me. I hear wailing and moaning. I'm being pulled upward! My little piece of the Animal Soul is being tugged. No! I won't go!

It pulls at me and I hold firm, with the crying all through my body. A sloth cannot be pulled from his branch. It passes on, leaving me alone.

"That was its first pass, little sloth. It'll come again."

"I don't want to die, Father! Why do I have to?"

"Our great departure time may have come. All the signs indicate that it has, but nonetheless it's our duty to resist. Hang on now, it comes once more. It's stronger now. It's gathered the jaguars to itself. They've surrendered. The great cats have all yielded. Now it springs at us . . . now . . ."

My limbs are trembling. I feel weak, drained, terrified. It strikes, leaping upon me like the cat, and rushes upward through my body, carrying my little bit of soul in its great teeth. My beautiful jungle! I don't want to leave. Oh lovely earth, please let me stay!

I hang fast as it leaps away. My blood is roaring, my heart crashing violently in my chest. "Oh, Master, I felt them all, felt the whole Soul rising. The whole Soul—what will happen if it takes me?"

"You won't be hanging upside down anymore."

"But will I continue somewhere?"

"Who knows?" The moss parts and I see the raindrop again. It has grown larger and the bits of leaf all around it are wet.

I hear the Soul moving through the jungle corridors, through the galleries and tunnels of our home. It rolls over me again and circles through every part of my body. I'm drawn into the depths of the Soul, into its vast dream. I've hung on for countless seasons. I've hung on through the ages. I'll hang on. This is my branch.

But it's all loosened. The whole thing's unraveling. So many threads cut today. Our link to the earth is broken. Jungle of happiness! Earth! My paws are slipping away from you. My billionfold claws are weak and trembling. The tail of the dog hangs dead; my horns are cracked, my trunk has been cut.

Ah, forest, my favorite glade! Deep and quiet cave, I shall miss you. And how shall I find you again? This path of my nature took so long to fashion and now—now it is undone, never to be found or fashioned again.

Tremendous, tremendous this Soul, with such secrets yet to unfold, but—the unfolding is over. We made our bid for existence and lost.

Leaving this pillow in the corner, where I went to wash my paws; leaving the sand box under the window where I buried my waste. Leaving the street where I smelled your signs. Turning round, I tremble on the floor, heaving my chest. Springing from the windows, shuddering on the lawn—in the jungle, in the cities, on the mountaintops, I groan.

And I must let go of my branch.

Crawling out from under all this rubbish and smoldering rubble. The bastards burned the laboratory down. I'm lucky to have gotten out alive. But Doctor Rat is made of tough stuff, my friends. I felt an awful tugging on my tail there for a moment and thought I was a goner, but I held onto a bound set of old Newsletters.

Pushing debris out of my way, crawling up over this pile of broken bricks. We'll have to requisition some funds in a hurry and rebuild the place.

Okay, Rat, just slip under this smoldering timber and . . .

. . . out in the moist night air. On the rolling campus lawn. It's awfully quiet out here. It feels so still. Kind of an eerie feeling. I must make note of it for my Displacement Behavior Paper.

There's the Central Exercise Drum in the ruins. Still spinning around. No rats in it; it's just clicking slowly over and over, running down. Still some signals from the intuitive band though. I'd better tune in and see what's become of the revolution.

Good heavens!

Gone? All of them? They couldn't be. I'd better change the channel. Pick up a stray dog somewhere and bring him back for the heatstroke study.

Panning the globe, from place to place. Piles of dead animals. Basic models in great heaps, already starting to rot. Get busy with the pickling solution, gentlemen.

This is remarkable. I can't find a single cur anywhere. Let's just focus down this Chinese alleyway, behind that restaurant, maybe we'll find a cat or two to put in the chow mein . . .

Empty. Not a puss anywhere.

Changing channels again . . . switch to India, they've got loads of monkeys there . . . in on Delhi, check out the trapping agencies . . . trappers pulling out their hair, wringing their hands, tossing ashes in their eyes . . . dead monkeys everywhere . . . not a tail stirring.

Try the education network—Learned Professors looking around dumbly . . . graduate assistants registering shock . . . stupefied stares. Every rat, every cat, every dog, every rabbit, every mouse, every mole, every chimp, every guinea pig dead!

"WHAT'S GOING TO HAPPEN TO OUR HEATSTROKE STUDY!"

No answer. The line is dead.

Exercise Drum coming to a stop, its momentum gone. The signal is fading away. Just a faint little blip in the middle of the screen, getting smaller and smaller, like a satellite disappearing into space.

Surely there must be a titmouse somewhere. Let me just spin the drum once more and see what I come up with. . . .

Empty. The place is deserted. There's not an animal anywhere on earth. Old Doctor Rat is the only one left.

Crawling over the stones, and into the shadows. The silence is rather unnerving (cf. Musgrave and Hamilton, *The Extinct Species*). Over. *Kaput.*

I hear people talking on campus; they sound unusually quiet. Humanity is still functioning. But no scurrying little feet in the grass. No softly sliding feline shadows. Not a single meow, not a chirp, not a solitary bark in the whole of creation. You can feel the emptiness out there: the Final Solution gives you a sort of lonely feeling.

And I haven't even got a place to live. Maybe I can find an old gopher hole somewhere.

Going along the sidewalk, dragging my tail.

ABOUT THE AUTHOR

WILLIAM KOTZWINKLE is a young writer who has already produced five books of fiction and nine children's books. His underground popularity is large and has been growing steadily. Among his books are *Elephant Bangs Train, The Fan Man* and *Swimmer in the Secret Sea. Doctor Rat,* an absolutely wonderful novel, both an indictment and a lyric celebration, will be the book that breaks him out "above ground." His most recent novel is *Fata Morgana.* Mr. Kotzwinkle has lived for several years in Canada.

RELAX!
SIT DOWN
and Catch Up On Your Reading!

Bantam Book Catalog

Here's your up-to-the-minute listing of every book currently available from Bantam.

This easy-to-use catalog is divided into categories and contains over 1400 titles by your favorite authors.

So don't delay—take advantage of this special opportunity to increase your reading pleasure.

Just send us your name and address and 25¢ (to help defray postage and handling costs).